SEX GOD

BY: MARIE FORCE

Published by HTJB, Inc.
Copyright 2017. HTJB, Inc.
Cover Design: Kristina Brinton
Interior Layout: Isabel Sullivan, E-Book Formatting Fairies

ISBN: 978-1946136138

www.marieforce.com

CHAPTER 1

Garrett

"I married the first man who made me come," Lauren says matter-of-factly, "and we all know how *that* turned out."

The chicken wing I'm about to stuff in my face is now suspended in midair as her words sink into my sex-starved brain. "*Wayne Peterson* was the first guy to make you come?"

"Don't judge me." She licks the barbecue sauce from her wing before she takes a dainty bite. I'm fascinated by the way she eats a wing without getting even a smudge of sauce on her lips, whereas I feel like I've taken a bath in the stuff. "I didn't even know what an orgasm was until Wayne gave me one."

Fascinated, I lean in closer. "How'd he do it?"

"Tongue," she says, also leaning in so she can't be overheard. In Marfa, Texas, someone is always listening. "I also didn't know people did...*that*...until Wayne did it to me."

This makes me laugh because she's so damned cute as she says it. "I was fourteen when I caught Tommy going down on Debbie in the basement family room. I had no idea what they were doing until I saw his tongue out and his face all slimy. She was squealing like a pig and pulling his hair. I thought it was the grossest thing I'd ever seen."

She sputters with laughter. "Oh my God! Did he know you saw them?"

"Nope." My brother, three years older than me, surely would've killed me, if for no other reason than I'd gotten an eyeful of his precious Debbie's bush and tits. They've been married close to ten years now and live in California, which means all the responsibility for my dad's business, our mother and younger siblings falls to me while my older brother lives large on the West Coast. That's a sore subject I try not to think too much about.

"Well, you were way ahead of me in figuring that one out."

Since she never, ever talks about the ex-husband who knocked her around on his way out of town to parts unknown, I take this opportunity to dig a little deeper. "So before it went bad with him, it was good?"

"Nah, it was never good. I think he made me come three times in total. He was always an asshole, but he didn't become a violent asshole until six months after I made the huge mistake of marrying him."

The thought of gigantic Wayne Peterson getting rough with tiny Lauren makes me fucking furious. "I hope you know there're a lot of guys in this town who'd love five minutes alone in a room with that son of a bitch."

She takes a drink from her bottle of Bud, her eyes shining warmly at me. "You're very sweet to say so."

"I mean it. If I ever lay eyes on that asshole again, I'll show him what it feels like to get the shit kicked out of him." And I could do it, too. I might push paper for a living, but I work out like a fiend. That's one of several ways I deal with the stress of being stuck in a life I never signed on for.

"How'd we get on this subject anyway?" she asks after a long silence.

With Lauren, silence is always comfortable. Neither of us feels the need to fill the void with pointless chatter. Our friendship is like a well-oiled machine, except in the bedroom, where it all fell apart the one time we tried to take this flirtation-slash-slow-burn-slash-unfulfilled-desire-that-is-ever-present between us to the next level.

How do you spell d-i-s-a-s-t-e-r?

Until that night six months ago, I hadn't known it was possible to do sex *wrong*. I don't like to brag, but the word "god" has often been used regarding my abilities between the sheets. Until I took Lauren to bed, I'd been the recipient of an endless streak of five-star reviews on my performance. But lo and behold, it's actually possible to get it so wrong you aren't sure if you'll ever again be able to look at the woman you've lusted after for years—while telling yourself you're "just" friends—in the aftermath of such calamity.

"I have no idea how we got on this subject," I reply as I shake off the disturbing memories.

"We were talking about orgasms," she reminds me.

The word "orgasms" reminds me of the dreadful encounter that threw a bucket of ice on our longtime slow burn for each other. There were no orgasms that night. "*You're* talking orgasms. I'm trying to eat my wings." Thank God we were able to salvage the friendship that means so much to both of us, not to mention our group of mutual friends.

Her best friend, Honey, got together with my close friend Blake last year, and they'd love to see us together, too. That isn't going to happen, but beer and wings on Mondays? That happens every week without fail. If I find myself living for Monday, well…

She laughs at my comment about trying to eat my wings. I love the sound of her laugh. There's something earthy and sexy and dirty about it. In truth, I love everything about her. I love the curly blonde hair that would look messy on another woman but suits her to perfection. I love her big brown eyes and how she's so honest that when she tries to lie about anything, she cries. I love that she spends as much time at the gym as I do and has the biceps to prove it. I adore the piercings that line her left ear and the butterfly tattoos that covers scars we never talk about on her inner wrists.

She loves butterflies. They're all over her house and the flower shop that she owns in town. They're sort of her trademark, along with the bright colors that decorate her and her surroundings. Tonight she's wearing a frilly orange top with white short-shorts. Not that I noticed her awesome legs and ass on the way in or anything...

The other thing I absolutely love about her is the way she looks at me as if I'm the guy she'd want if she could have her pick of all the men in the world. If I were looking for a forever kind of woman, Lauren would be at the top of my list of candidates. In fact, she'd be the only candidate. But the last thing I want, after years of endless responsibility, is a serious relationship or anything that would permanently tie me to Marfa. She owns a home and a business here. Getting involved with Lauren on a more serious level than as best friends would definitely tie me to Marfa, and that's my biggest hesitation where she's concerned.

"Sometimes, I think it's me," she says softly. "Like there's something wrong with me."

This stuns me even more than hearing Wayne fucking Peterson was the first guy to make her come. "What do you mean?"

She looks so defeated that I want to reach across the table to offer comfort, but I can't seem to move my arms or anything else for that matter. "When a girl starts to string together enough disastrous sexual encounters, she begins to wonder if *she's* the problem."

"That's ridiculous. It's not *you*. You're just picking the wrong guys."

She gives me a look filled with skepticism. "Including you?"

I'm riveted by the first mention either of us has made of that awful night when everything that could go wrong did. "That was an off night, and it was more my fault than yours."

She sweeps away my comment with her hand. "You're just saying that because you're a good friend, and you're trying to make me feel better."

"That is *not* why I said it, and it *was* my fault."

"Why do you think that?" she asks, looking adorably perplexed.

I've given this a lot of thought in the months that have passed since that night, and I've come to some conclusions. "First of all, I was freaked out about ruining our friendship, which messed with my head. Both of them, actually. Second, we did it all wrong."

"There's a *wrong* way?" she asks, her brows rising in amazement.

"Hell yes, there's a wrong way. We rushed over the preliminaries. I didn't take my time. I got naked with you five minutes after the first time I kissed you. That's not how it should be done when two people have as much history between them as we do."

The truth of the matter is I'd wanted her naked and horizontal in a bed with me for so long that when opportunity knocked the first time, I pounced like a hormonal teenage boy rather than the experienced man that I am. I've sorely regretted that ever since—even more so now that I know she's been blaming herself. "It shouldn't have happened that way. You deserve so much better than what you got from me. I think you are..."

"What?" she asks again in that sweet, sexy tone. "What am I?"

"You're *everything*," I whisper gruffly.

"Except compatible with you in bed," she reminds me with the kind of bluntness I expect from her. We talk about *everything*. See Exhibit A above—orgasms.

I clear my throat and decide to take a dive that's been six long, torturous months in the making, since the ill-fated night with her put a serious hit on my sexual GPA. "I really think we ought to try again." I actually hadn't had that thought until I heard that she thinks she's the problem. I absolutely can't have her thinking that when it's not true. Before I pick up stakes and head out of this godforsaken town, I need to prove otherwise to her, if it's the last thing I do.

Before the words are even all the way out of my mouth, her head is shaking—and not in a good way. "I can't bear to be humiliated like that again."

"I like to think we were equally humiliated, and at the end of the day, it's just me and you here, Lauren."

"And maybe we're better as best friends."

"I'm not ready to accept that after one failed attempt."

"Garrett..." The pleading edge to her voice makes me feel like an ass for forcing her to talk about it. "We were so lucky to get past that and to put this back on track." She gestures to the plate of wings and the bottles of beer on the table.

Forgetting where we are and that half the town is probably watching, I reach across the table for her hand. I need to touch her. For the longest time, she's been the brightest light in my life. Why? I can't say exactly. Except for the one night we tried to have more, we've only ever been the best of friends. All I know is that I can't leave her with any thoughts of her own inadequacy—especially if I've contributed to them in any way. "Give me one week to prove it's not you. That's all I'm asking."

"But what if we really are better off as friends than..."

"Lovers?"

She cringes and wrinkles her cute little nose. "That's such a gross word."

Laughing, I say, "What would you call it?"

"Friends with benefits?"

"I can live with that description. I want another chance, Lauren. Let me show you what can happen when we savor rather than devour."

She draws in a shaky-sounding deep breath, and her face flushes with a rosy glow that has my cock stirring.

"What do you say?"

She takes a drink from her beer bottle. Even that seems insanely sexy in light of our conversation. "How would it work, this so-called week where you prove it's not me?" Is her voice huskier than usual, or is that wishful thinking on my part?

I've thought about what went wrong that night from every possible angle, and I've realized that a longer, more drawn-out seduction is what we should've done then—and it's what we'll do this time, if she gives me another chance. "You'd have to trust me with the details. I wouldn't want you to worry about anything. Leave it all to me."

"Under one condition."

"Name it."

"No matter what happens, you promise me we'll still have this after." Again, she gestures to the wings and beers, acting as a metaphor for our friendship.

"You have my word. Do I have yours?" I want her to know the friendship is as important to me as it is to her. "No matter what happens, we still have this?"

"Absolutely."

"Is that a yes, then?"

She nods. "I'm willing to try again if you're so sure it won't be another disaster."

I'm not sure of anything other than I want another chance. "Tomorrow night, I'll pick you up at seven. I want you to wear the sexiest dress you own with nothing under it. Oh, and heels. I want some sky-high heels, too. Can you do that?"

Her mouth drops open in shock. I can't wait to see those plump lips wrapped around my cock. We didn't get to that the first time around. We'll definitely get there next time. "Lauren?"

"Um, yes, okay. I can do that."

I signal for our check, throw a fifty on it and stand to leave. We came separately, but next time, we'll come together. I almost laugh at my own joke. Bending, I brush a kiss over her rosy cheek. "See you tomorrow."

After I leave her, I wonder how long she sat there with her mouth hanging open over my audacious instructions. I can't wait for tomorrow night.

*

I have a confession to make. I fucking hate Marfa. Sure, it was an okay place to grow up, but it was never my plan to be stuck in the middle of buttfuck nowhere West Texas as an adult. We're three hours to El Paso to the west, five, six and eight hours respectively to San Antonio, Austin and Houston to the east, and seven and a half hours to Dallas to the north. In short, Marfa is next to nothing but wide-open desert.

I went to college at Texas A&M, eight hours from Marfa in College Station, between Austin and Houston, and spent many a wild weekend in both cities. At the end of my senior year, I was entertaining job offers in several big Texas cities when the unthinkable happened. My dad dropped dead at work.

He was so proud of me for following him into accounting and boasted of my three-point-nine GPA to all his colleagues. We were consulting daily about the job offers I'd received and had narrowed it down to an oil company and a *Fortune* 500 corporation with offices all over the world. The plan was to start "local," meaning anywhere in Texas, and end up somewhere awesome. Dad was pushing me in the corporate direction over the always-volatile oil industry.

Until one night he didn't come home from work on time, and my mom went looking for him. She found him hunched over his desk, his body already cold and rigid. An autopsy determined he'd been dead about three hours by the time she found him.

Just that quickly, my plans changed, and all my choices were taken from me along with the father I worshipped. I did what was expected—and desperately needed—by coming home to run my father's local accounting business, the same business that supported my mom and the three younger siblings who were heading to college in the next few years.

This is one of many reasons I resent my older brother, who has been more than happy to leave all the responsibility for our family to good old Garrett while he and his wife, Debbie, have the time of their lives in California, or so it seems to me from the pictures they post constantly on Facebook. Every one of those pictures made me want to rip his face off for the first couple of years after my dad died, until I decided to let go of the bitterness that was eating me up inside. It wasn't Tommy's fault that our father died, or that I was the most qualified to take over the family business. At least, that's what I tell myself so I won't actually murder him on one of his infrequent visits.

Six years later, I've gotten an MBA through an online program and tripled the annual gross revenue of my father's small-town practice. I act as chief financial officer and/or controller for most of the major businesses in town. Ever since my father died, I've had the same plan—get my younger siblings through college, set my mom up for retirement, sell the business to some enterprising CPA looking to step into a successful practice, and then *finally* go see to the plans that were put on hold for six long years.

Last year, my staff of seven and I cleared a million dollars in net revenue. For the non-accountants out there, that's *after* expenses. That cool million means I have the tuition I need for my sisters and can set my mom up royally. This week I got a phone call from a headhunter I've been working with for a year as I test the waters to see what else might be out there for me now that I've fulfilled my obligations to my family. He's set up an interview with a huge tech company in Austin for this weekend, and he said they want me bad. It sure does feel good to be wanted.

I'd be on my way out of Marfa forever if it wasn't for one small, niggling detail named Lauren Davies, who also happens to own one of the few businesses in Marfa that *doesn't* use the services of Garrett McKinley, CPA.

I've had my theories as to why, theories that were confirmed on that one ill-fated night we spent in her bed in which everything that could go wrong did. She confessed that the chemistry that's always simmered on a low boil between us stopped her from hiring me to handle her accounting. Turns out, that was probably a savvy move on her part, because the first time we decided to test that chemistry in the lab, so to speak, we created a disaster of epic proportions. I shudder thinking about my first-ever case of performance anxiety that led to one fumbling attempt after another to successfully close the deal.

Ugh. I can't bear to remember it. Except... One shining memory stands out in a sea of things I'd rather forget—the visual of Lauren's spectacular naked body that is so seared into my brain it'll never be forgotten.

As I sit in the office in the much larger building I moved the business to three years after dad died, visions of naked Lauren dance like sugarplums through my addled brain, especially after last night's conversation about orgasms. Thinking about giving her an orgasm has me hard as concrete *in my office, in the middle of the freaking workday.*

If I made a spreadsheet of Lauren's attributes, it would look something like this:

1. Smooth, lightly tanned skin.
2. Big, full breasts with light brown nipples made for sucking.
3. A flat, toned belly.
4. Endless, sexy legs.
5. A completely bare pussy (or as I like to think of it—the frosting on a delicious piece of cake).
6. A perfect ass that makes me want to grab on and do dirty, dirty things.
7. Gorgeous brown eyes.
8. Curly blonde hair that I want to wrap around my hands when I fuck her from behind.
9. A mouth made for sin, and I have a few specific sins in mind when it comes to her luscious mouth.

Total = Perfection.

I lick my lips as I catalog every spectacular detail of her stunning body. Of course, I've always known she's hot as fuck. We grew up together. I've seen her in everything from a bikini to a prom gown to the shortest of skirts and the highest of heels. But seeing her in absolutely nothing was a revelation. Literally. And figuratively. I'm never sure of the proper use of those two words, so let me sum it up—Lauren Davies is a literal and figurative smoking-hot babe.

Tonight I'm going to prove to her that her challenges with guys have nothing at all to do with her and everything to do with *them*. Once I get her feeling better about herself, I'm so outta here.

CHAPTER 2

Garrett

At this point, you might be wondering what a guy who doesn't want to put down roots in the small town where he feels stuck does about sex when he's not creating a sexual disaster with his best friend. One word: tourists. They come from all over to see Marfa's famous lights, the art installations and to soak up the funky artsy vibe of our desert town. They're easy to find in the bars and restaurants around town, and it doesn't take much effort to convince one of them to invite me to her hotel room for some mindless fun.

Since I returned home after college, I've "honed my craft," if you will, with tourists. The beauty of the transient encounter is that they don't know any of my people, so they don't talk and they don't spread rumors that might get back to those who might be appalled by my tourist trade. I send my out-of-towners away with smiles on their faces and good memories of their brief visit to Marfa. I don't give them my last name or phone number, so there's never a chance of a repeat performance. It may sound shallow, but it's worked to keep me sane when so much of my existence is out of my control.

Around town, I have a reputation for being somewhat of a monk, focused exclusively on running my thriving business while helping my mom and acting like a surrogate dad to my three younger siblings. I like that reputation. I love that my friends think I do without. It makes me laugh. I like that no one knows about the tourists that have kept me from actually living like a monk while I wait and hope for something better than my life in Marfa.

Lauren and our tight-knit group of friends have been a bright spot in my life since I came home after college. It's been a couple of years now since the night Lauren's argument with Wayne turned violent. I'll never forget receiving the call from Honey with the news that Lauren was in the hospital, badly beaten by her husband. I wanted to murder Wayne with my own hands, but because so many people depend on me, I resisted that urge and focused all my attention on Lauren. I visited her for hours every day for the week she was hospitalized, and after she was released, I spent fourteen nights on her sofa so she wouldn't have to be home alone at night.

Her closest girlfriends, Honey, Julie and Scarlett, volunteered to stay with her, but she wanted me. Probably because she knew I'd beat the living shit out of Wayne if he came anywhere near her. I still hope to get the chance to teach him a lesson about what happens to guys who treat women the way he did Lauren.

She's been understandably fragile since that incident. That's why I've never pushed her for more than the close friendship we've always shared. Instead, I've bided my time, fucked tourists, hung out with my friends, worked out seven days a week at the local gym, focused on growing my business and taking care of my family—always with the end goal of getting the fuck out of here the very second my youngest sister graduates from high school. That's happening in three short weeks, and I'm counting down the days. I've even talked to a Realtor about putting my house on the market the day my sister, Sierra, graduates. My "baby" sister plans to join our other sister, Lola, at UT in Austin in the fall, and I've got both their tuitions covered, along with generous monthly allowances that keep them in their favorite things, including lip gloss, nail polish and heels.

So that's pretty much been my life in a nutshell—work, family, the gym, tourists and friends. Nothing overly exciting or out of the routine until six months ago, when a regular beer-and-wings night turned into something far from ordinary with Lauren. For one thing, she wore a frilly floral yellow dress that showed off her considerable cleavage. And for some reason, her curly hair was unusually orderly and she applied makeup that did crazy things to her big eyes.

But it wasn't just her appearance that was different that night. She was also flirtatious with me, looking at me with something far more complicated than friendship and touching me every chance she got. It reminded me of the old days, before she lost her mind and married Wayne fucking Peterson. And by the way, I blame myself for the fact that she married him in the first place, but I'll tell you about that later.

Anyway, I could tell from the minute she walked into our usual meeting spot that she was looking to bust loose a little that night. So I indulged her. I let her drink a lot more than she normally does, intending to see her safely home. We shot pool and danced and generally had a freaking blast.

In hindsight, I can see that I was so fucking relieved to see the sparkle back in her eyes that I got caught up in the magic she spun around us that night. I thought, finally... After all this time, we're going to get *our* chance. For a guy who prides himself on understanding women, God, did I get it wrong that night.

I still cringe when I think about taking her home and kissing her the way I'd wanted to for so long, right on her front porch where anyone might've seen us. That kiss... I've thought about that kiss every day for six months. It was the best kiss I've ever had with anyone, and it made me want so much more. Without taking even so much as a minute to think about consequences, I had her inside and pressed against the door as I continued to devour her like a man who'd been starving for a taste of this one particular woman.

We pulled at clothes, both of us seeming equally desperate for the feel of skin on skin. The entire thing was surreal, as if it was happening in one of my many Lauren-related fantasies instead of transpiring in real life. Somehow I knew that if I took even half a second to ask her if she was sure this was what she wanted that the bubble would burst and the magic would be lost. So I pressed on, even as a niggling feeling of concern made me question whether we'd be risking a friendship we both relied upon by letting this happen.

We ended up in her bedroom, still kissing furiously with years of latent desire bursting forth explosively. She took my breath away, leaving me light-headed from the lack of oxygen. Breathing would mean breaking the kiss, and there was no way I was going to do that. My hands were everywhere—in her hair, on her breasts, cupping her sweet ass. I'd never wanted anyone or anything the way I wanted her in that moment.

I recall being mesmerized by her soft skin, gorgeous breasts, light brown nipples and the totally bare pussy that was a delightful surprise and made me drool with years of pent-up lust for her. Everything was going great until I stopped kissing her long enough to remove my pants and underwear.

She took one look at my hard cock, and the bubble burst.

I wasn't sure if she recoiled out of fear or horror, or what happened, but she punched out of what had been about to happen, leaving me reeling as I tried to catch up.

"Lauren," I said, reaching for her. "What's wrong?"

She shook her head.

I stretched out next to her and put my arm around her, alarmed to discover she was trembling violently. "Did I do something to scare you, sweetheart?" After what she'd been through, that would kill me.

"N-no. I, um… I'm sorry. I didn't mean to do that." She turned to face me and started kissing me again, as if nothing had happened.

"Lauren—"

"Please, Garrett. This is what I want. Please don't stop."

I try to be a good guy and always aim to do the right thing, but I'm only human. When a woman I care about as much as I do Lauren begs me to make love to her, I'm going to give her what she wants, even if I'm not one hundred percent certain it's the right thing to do.

So I started all over again with desperate kisses while I caressed her breasts and teased her nipples. Then I kissed her jaw and rolled her earlobe between my teeth, loving the gasp of surprise that drew from her. Encouraged by her reactions, I moved down, cupping her left breast and drawing her nipple into my mouth.

She cried out from the sensations, and I sucked harder, wanting to erase anything upsetting or negative from her mind and replace it with pure pleasure. I gave her other breast the same treatment and then kissed her abdomen until she was fairly wriggling under me, all but begging for more.

When I settled her legs on my shoulders, I noticed she was still trembling violently. I almost stopped to ask again if this was what she wanted, but she'd told me what she wanted, and I was determined to give it to her. Dropping my head, I traced her outer lips with my tongue before delving inside to lap up her sweetness. Goddamn, she was like a drug. One taste and I was addicted.

I went a little crazy in my efforts to make her come, licking and sucking and driving my fingers into her tight, wet channel, but I couldn't seem to get her there, which should've been the first clue that this was going south fast. I only stopped long enough to roll on a condom and began to press into her, slowly and carefully, aware that it had been a while since she'd done this.

For a few minutes, anyway, everything seemed okay, but then I sensed her checking out again, like she'd done earlier.

I stopped, gazing down at her, looking for a sign of how I should proceed. That was when I saw tears rolling into her hair. My erection shriveled up and died at the sight of those tears. "Lauren…"

"I'm so sorry," she said on a sob. "I don't know what's wrong with me."

I withdrew, stretched out next to her and tried to offer comfort I wasn't sure she wanted. "There is *nothing* wrong with you." I began to wonder if maybe there was something wrong with *me*. More than one of my tourists have told me I'm a "sex god." Before that ill-fated night, I had never been with a woman who didn't come—multiple times—with me.

How could I fail so spectacularly with the only woman who ever really mattered? That question still haunts me to this day.

"Tonight wasn't our night," I told her at the time. "Doesn't mean anything."

Our friends had been waiting hopefully for a long time to hear we were officially together. After that night, the announcement never came. It was like we took a hundred steps backward, which made it that much easier to ramp up my plans to move on from Marfa. The thought of maybe, possibly, someday with her had been the single thread keeping me tied to my hometown, but that thread was severed that night. It wasn't going to happen with her, and I was strangely fine with that, but only because it reduced the complications, not because I didn't still want her. Of course, I did. Even more so after having seen her gorgeous naked body.

I've spent many an hour thinking about the things we did that night. Remembering her light brown nipples, her bare pussy, the taste of her desire and the tight squeeze of her internal muscles around my cock has led to many a session in the shower to find some relief from the images that plague me.

But what's been really strange is that I haven't gone near any of the usual tourist hot spots since that night with Lauren. I've been living up to my reputation as a monk, having lost the desire to be with other women after being with her—even if the encounter was a mess.

For weeks afterward, the possibility that I might've done something to set her back ate at me. It took me a month or so to realize that neither of us did anything wrong that night. She simply wasn't ready to go "there" with me. Once I made peace with that, I relaxed about it somewhat but not completely.

I felt a thousand times better when she texted me two weeks later to resume our beer-and-wings date, which took place the following Monday with nary a reference to the sex gone bad. Six long months have passed without us talking about it. And in those months, I've watched her slowly but surely come back to the Lauren she was before Wayne attacked her—funny, gutsy, audacious, flirty and sexy as all fuck.

Sometimes I thought I might go out of my mind waiting for her to get back to normal so I could feel better about leaving town. I've always known that she depends on me. With everything falling into place with my company and my family, I should feel completely guilt-free about moving forward with my plans. But after hearing that Lauren thinks *she* is the problem when it comes to sex, I'm riddled with guilt about leaving before I fix that misconception.

Now that she's given me this week to show her that there's absolutely nothing wrong with her, I'm determined to get it three thousand percent right. I leave work early to make preparations to ensure a successful evening. That's what I did wrong the last time. I didn't prepare properly or see to the details. Normally, I'm all for spontaneity. But what works with my tourists is not what Lauren needs, especially after what Wayne put her through. She's probably expecting me to feed and ravish her, and though that's exactly what I *want* to do, there'll be no ravishing tonight. Well, maybe a little ravishing, but that isn't the overall goal of this evening.

No, the only thing that will get laid tonight is groundwork. We're going to build up to the main event, and by the time I get her there at the end of the week, I want her so desperate and so needy that nothing—and I do mean *nothing*—will get in the way of the best sex she's ever had. I've waited this long to move on with my life. Devoting this week to Lauren won't hurt anything, especially if it means giving her the peace she so richly deserves at the end.

Lauren

I finish the orders that have come into my flower shop, Bloomsbury, by two o'clock and leave the store in the reliable hands of Megan, the high school girl who has worked for me for two years now. A few doors down the street, I pop into my friend Honey's photography studio.

"Be right out," she calls after the bells on the door announce my arrival.

"It's just me."

"Oh good! Come on back."

I walk through the wide-open space that Honey uses to shoot her Desert Babies portraits. Families come from all over Texas for her distinctive photos that feature babies in the desert environment that surrounds Marfa. In the office, I find

Honey seated at her desk, feet up and keyboard on her lap. "Thank goodness it's just you. I'm so comfortable, and that's a rare thing these days."

Honey's pregnant belly seems to get bigger every day. "How is my nephew doing?" I drop into one of her visitor chairs.

She lays her hand over the baby bump. "I think he's playing rugby today."

"Ouch."

"You said it. The feet to the ribs are my favorite."

"Won't be long now, Mama."

"I can't wait. Blake is so excited. He talks to him every night and tells him all the things he's going to teach him."

"It's great to see him so happy." During our senior year of high school, Blake was devastated by the loss of his girlfriend, Jordan, in a car that he was driving when a truck broadsided it. He's never been the same, and only after he fell in love with Honey last year did he seem to recover somewhat. "Both of you deserve everything you've got now."

Honey gives me an odd look. "What's the matter?"

"Why would you ask me what's wrong when I'm saying you and Blake deserve to be happy?"

"Because I know you, and as much as I appreciate that, I can tell when you're upset about something."

That's the thing about meeting your best friends in kindergarten. No one knows you like they do. "I'm not upset... I'm anxious."

"About?"

"I have a date with Garrett tonight. A real date, not the usual beer and wings."

Honey lets out a giddy squeal and claps her hands. "It's about freaking time!" She puts the keyboard on her desk and drops her feet to the floor so she can lean in for closer scrutiny. "What brought this on? We all assumed you guys decided to just stay friends."

"We did. We *had*. We... Well, it's complicated."

"How so?"

I bite my lip while trying to decide how much to tell my best friend, who is also Garrett's good friend. "We sort of had sex six months ago."

Honey stares at me, eyes agog. "How can you *sort of* have sex?"

"We did it, but it was weird and awkward and well... not good."

"Ohhhh." Honey taps her bottom lip. "This is extremely surprising in light of his... well..."

"Reputation?"

Nodding, Honey says, "Supposedly, he's somewhat of a... um..."

"God in bed?" Girls we knew growing up used to wax poetic about his skills even when we were still in high school. Garrett thinks we don't know this, but Honey and I are well aware that more than one tourist has come to town for a roll in the sack with the guy known as the Sex God.

"Yes! So, what the hell went so wrong?"

"I have no idea. I've gone over it and over it in my mind a million times, but it never makes sense. I adore him, and vice versa. We've been hot for each other for ages. It should've been off the charts. Instead, it barely made the chart, and it brought back a lot of crap from when I was with Wayne and he would tell me I suck in bed."

"Wayne is an asshole, and you do *not* suck in bed."

"How do you know that?" I ask with a laugh.

"Because you're gorgeous and sexy and any man would be lucky to have you in his bed."

The fear that Wayne is right about me has been keeping me awake at night since the disaster with Garrett. Though I'm touched by Honey's unwavering love for me, I go with sarcasm to hide my emotional response. "And you're not even slightly impartial."

"Not at all. It's a well-known fact that men who suck in bed frequently make their partners feel responsible for their inadequacies. Clearly, Wayne passed off his own failings onto you, and you can't let him get away with that."

"Where did you hear this well-known fact?"

"*Cosmo.* Where else?"

Snorting with laughter, I say, "Of course. Where else, indeed." I run my hands over the skirt of my dress as another thought occurs to me. "But what if Wayne was right and I *do* suck in bed? What if it was my fault that it went so badly with Garrett?"

"Lauren! Stop this! It wasn't you. It was an off night. I can't stand to see you doing this to yourself. If you believe that crap, then Wayne wins, and he can't ever win. I won't allow it."

Honey's fierce defense goes a long way toward making me feel better, but I won't truly believe it wasn't me until Garrett and I successfully close the deal.

"What I want to know is *why* you didn't tell me about this before now."

"Because it was so embarrassing. It took six months for us to even talk about that night."

"At least you've managed to stay friends. Thank goodness for that."

"Yes, thank goodness." A falling-out between Garrett and me would be a nightmare, not just for us but for our close circle of friends, too.

"So why are you so tightly wound today if this happened six months ago?"

"Last night, when we finally talked about it, Garrett said he wants a do-over. He thinks we went about it all wrong last time."

"Wow. How do you feel about that?"

"I'm afraid it'll be more of the same, and we'll actually ruin a rather spectacular friendship this time."

"Hmmm." Honey gave that some thought.

"What does that mean? Hmmm?"

"All of us—me, Blake, Matt, Julie, Scarlett—think you two would be a great couple."

"Why do you say that?"

"For one thing, you're already close friends. For another, you're attracted to him, and vice versa. Anyone with two working eyes can see that. Whenever we're all together, you always end up sitting next to him. You finish each other's sentences and laugh at all the same things. He holds doors for you and dotes on you. You guys already act like a couple."

"We do?" I'm stunned by Honey's observations. "I've never noticed we do any of that stuff. It's just me and Garrett being me and Garrett."

"Exactly—and you two are already a couple in many of the most important ways."

"Except *the* most important way." I can't bear to think about our fumbling attempt at sex. "I'm so nervous about it happening again. I'd be lost without him as a friend."

"Forget about that night. Tonight is a fresh start. Wipe the slate clean and pretend like the first time never happened. It was one night out of a whole lifetime. Bad sex happens."

"Has it ever happened to you with Blake?"

"Umm, well, Blake is a very unique exception to all rules."

"I know. I remember. What does it say that I had better sex with Garrett's friend years ago than I had with him?"

"It says you're reminding me that you once had sex with my husband, which we've agreed to never talk about."

I laugh at the face she makes at me. "It was more than once."

"And you didn't have any problems with him, did you?"

"No, but that was more about him than me. As you well know, he's rather good at it."

"So is Garrett by all accounts. Has it occurred to you that maybe it's more complicated with him because you have genuine feelings for him, which you didn't have for Blake? Because if you did, I'd have to kill you."

Laughing, I say, "No need for murder. I love Blake to pieces, as you well know, but it was just sex with him."

"It's very possible that you and Garrett haven't hit your stride yet, and you will. How can you not? You're you—gorgeous and sexy—and he's smoking hot, intense, has all those muscles and is a known sex god. I'd be more afraid of what's going to happen when you get it right than I would be of getting it wrong again. You're apt to burn down the house together."

"If that happens, I hope we end up at his place rather than mine. I bet he has better insurance than I do."

Honey laughs. "Relax and enjoy the company of one of your favorite people. Think of it as just another night with Garrett. If you build it up to be a huge big deal in your mind, you'll set yourself up for disaster."

"Too late for the warning about building it up to be a huge big deal."

Honey hauls herself up and out of the desk chair. It's almost painful to watch her try to move with the giant baby belly weighing down her petite frame. She comes around the desk and reaches for my hands, drawing me up and into a hug that's hampered by that big old belly.

"This is *Garrett*. He loves you. He'd do anything for you. You have nothing in the world to worry about."

"Except making things weird with one of my best friends."

She draws back from me, but leaves her hands on my shoulders. "You got past the weirdness once before. You can do it again, if it comes to that."

"Maybe it would be better…"

"What would be better?"

"If we just… If we didn't try to make it more than it already is."

"Is that what you want?"

I give that question careful consideration. I'm well aware of Garrett's affection for me. His devotion after the awful end of my marriage was more than I could've asked of any friend, and his steady presence in my life is something I count among my greatest blessings. But do I see us having more than great friendship?

"I'm not sure," I say in answer to my question and Honey's. "But I'd like to find out, if for no other reason than I'd like to put this 'will we or won't we' question to bed once and for all—pun intended."

She smiles and straightens my hair. "I want you to relax and put aside your worries and have a great time tonight, and then tomorrow call me and tell me every single detail."

I flash a coy grin. "I don't kiss and tell."

"This time you do. Remember how you made me tell you every detail of my first night with Blake?"

"I seem to recall something about that."

"Turnabout is fair play."

"Please don't say anything about this to Blake. I don't know what Garrett has told him, and I wouldn't want Garrett to think I'm blabbing about our personal business."

"Not to worry. My lips are sealed." Honey hugs me again, and this time I feel a strong kick from the baby against my abdomen.

"Holy cow! The kid's got game."

"I'm slightly afraid he's going to be a holy terror."

"I can't wait to meet him."

"Me either. Any day now."

"You'd better call me the second you go into labor, day or night."

"I will. Have a great time tonight, and don't forget to call me in the morning, or after lunch, or whatever time you two come up for air."

At the thought of an all-night sexfest with Garrett, my nipples tighten and my sex tingles. Apparently, my thoughts are stamped all over my face, because Honey loses it laughing. "All indications point toward this evening going much better than you think it will."

"Stop making fun of me," I toss over my shoulder as I leave her office to the sound of her laughter following me. I can't help but smile. I deserve her infectious laughter after the wide range of emotions I just displayed in the span of thirty minutes.

I'm a hot mess over this "date" with Garrett, but he'll never know that. Having taken the rest of the afternoon off, I head home to get ready—or as ready as I'll ever be to take another ride on the Garrett train.

CHAPTER 3

Garrett

The last item on my to-do list before I turn my focus to the evening with Lauren is a meeting with Blake Dempsey. He's been considering building some spec houses and asked me to do a cash-flow analysis before he decides his next step.

Since Blake is working outside of town at the site of the proposed development, I offer to go to him. I never miss a chance to get out of the office, so when my clients need me to come to them, I'm always happy to oblige. That's one part of my strategy to keep from going stir-crazy.

Today, I'm behind the wheel of the black Mercedes-Benz E Class sedan I treated myself to after our banner year. I'm as good of a good old boy as the next Texas guy, and I love my pickup, but every so often, a day calls for luxury. As I press the accelerator closer to the floor, I revel in the roar of the engine and the smoothness of the ride. I fucking love this car.

On the way to Blake's work site, I review the plans I made for the night with Lauren—lobster, her favorite food ever, flown in from Maine at an ungodly price, the best champagne I could get in town, flowers I bought from her shop after she left for the day and a plan that will begin tonight and conclude with the best sex of our lives later this week.

I've already told myself that no matter how hot she looks—and she will look *incredible*, of that I have no doubt—I will not take her to bed tonight. No, tonight and every night we spend together for the next few days will be about building the anticipation for the main event. With so much at stake, there's no room for another calamity. I've got to get it right this time.

Since I made the plans with Lauren last night, I haven't had much time to think about the incredibly enticing job lead with an Austin-based tech company that the headhunter has found for me. As I drive on the long, empty roads outside of town, I allow my mind to wander a little in that direction. The job I kiss her and hold her, that feeling is exactly the sort of thing I've been hoping for since I started looking again. The headhunter has come to me with quite a few things that didn't interest me. This one interests me tremendously.

While I enjoy being my own boss, it would be nice to have less responsibility for the overall business. What would it be like, I wonder, to put in a day at the office and then forget about the place until the next morning? I can barely recall what that's like, because I haven't had that kind of job since I worked at the local pizza place in high school.

I take good care of my clients. I'm available to them twenty-four-seven. I rarely take a full day off, even on weekends, which I use to catch up on the details of my own business, which gets overlooked while I'm busy all week helping others tend to their businesses.

It's a never-ending cycle of work, work and more work. That's not to say I don't enjoy it, because I do. Every day I'm presented with a different challenge in any number of a wide range of industries—from construction to photography to restaurants to hotels to dry cleaning and art galleries, among others. My clients help keep my life interesting, and I'm grateful for the trust they place in me.

But still… I dream about the opportunities that got away. Where would I be today if my father hadn't died? Would I be the CFO of a major US corporation, or would I have opened my own firm at some point? Where would I live? Austin? San Antonio? Houston? Or would I have left Texas by now for New York, Chicago or maybe Los Angeles? Would I be married with kids or still single?

The push-pull of what might have been versus what *is* continues to be a vexing debate that I keep entirely to myself. No one in my life knows how I really feel about having my professional choices taken from me due to the sudden death of my beloved father. What point is there to talking about it? It's not like there's anything I or my family or friends can do to change anything. And besides, I'd look like an ungrateful asshole if I complained about being forced to take over my dad's successful business, which became more so on my watch.

Poor me, right?

Since I don't want people to think I'm an ungrateful douche canoe, I keep my mouth shut and soldier on, even if the gnawing discontent is ever present in my daily life.

I hang a right onto a dirt road that leads into the development where Blake is working on the third of what will be thirty houses when the neighborhood is completed. My grade school friend's booming company is one of my bigger clients, and I couldn't be happier for his hard-earned success. Fueled by grief after the accident that took Jordan's life, Blake poured his heart and soul into growing the company into the powerhouse it is today.

Since he married Honey, Blake has been better about turning over some of the day-to-day management to his longtime foremen, including our friend Matt, but he still makes all the big decisions.

I park in the future driveway of the McMansion currently under construction. Bringing several file folders with me, I make my way inside, where Blake and his team are hanging drywall on the first floor. I feel like a fish out of water in my black pants, light blue dress shirt and Ferragamo loafers.

When Blake sees me, he hands off the nail gun to one of his employees before coming over to greet me with a handshake. "How's it going?"

"Good, you?"

"Great. We're making excellent progress here today."

"Progress is good."

"You want a tour?"

"Sure."

Blake walks me through the framed house, pointing out rooms that would soon be a family room, kitchen, formal living and dining rooms, an office, master suite and four additional bedrooms upstairs. "There'll be five bedrooms and six bathrooms and a media room in the basement."

As I follow Blake through the house, the oddest sensation comes over me. *This would be a great house to raise a family.* Where in the ever-loving fuck did that come from? I shake off the weird feeling and say all the right things to my friend and client, who is understandably proud of the work his company has done so far on this development.

"Is this one sold?"

"Yep, the first fifteen are spoken for. The other fifteen are the ones I'm thinking about building on spec in the hope that this'll become the next big neighborhood."

"With the town building a school out here, you've got a sure thing on your hands." I hand him the report I put together to evaluate the pros and cons of taking on the spec houses.

"Appreciate you driving out here to get this to me."

"Not a problem. If I waited for you to check your email, we'd never get anything done."

"This is true," Blake says with a laugh. He laughs often these days, thanks to his happy marriage. We're all thankful to have the Blake we used to know back with us after years of hell following Jordan's death.

"More pros than cons in the report," I tell him.

"I'll take a look and get back to you with questions. My biggest hesitation is taking on more with the baby due any time now."

"You've got good people working for you. At the rate you're growing, you're either going to need to hire a full-time business manager or take it on yourself."

He groans. "I hate that shit. I want to be on the job sites, not stuck in an office."

"Then maybe it's time to recruit for some executive-level help. The more you can delegate, the more you can get done in a day." We've already had this discussion several times in the last year.

"I know, I know. I'm thinking more about it with the baby coming. I want to be able to spend more time at home, and the only way I can do that is to bring in some help."

"Let me know when you're ready to pull the trigger, and I'll hook you up with a top recruiting firm."

"Go ahead and get me the info on the recruiters. We'll go from there."

"Wow, this is a big moment. I feel like there ought to be champagne or fireworks or *something* to celebrate."

"Very funny," he says with a good-natured grin. "You've worn me down."

"Then my work here is finished. I'll get some info together for you, and I'll help you find the right person."

"I was hoping you'd say that. I don't know the first thing about hiring a business manager."

"I gotcha covered."

"I know I say this all the time, but I couldn't do this without you, man. I'd have run the business into the ground without your advice and support."

"No way," I say with a laugh as a twinge of guilt hits me in the gut. What will my friend think of my get-out-of-Marfa plans? Though I know I'm good at my job, I also know that no one is irreplaceable. I'll find someone great to take over the local business if I get the job in Austin. "You got this."

"No, I really don't. *We've* got this. You and me."

The guilt hits me like a tsunami this time. If Blake or my other clients suspected that I long to be anywhere other than Marfa, Texas, it would create chaos in my carefully cultivated business life. So I'll keep my feelings on the topic to myself until I'm ready to unveil the plan for my departure that will include a replacement ready to take over where I leave off.

"I've got to roll," I tell Blake. "Talk to you tomorrow."

"Yes, you will."

He sees me off, and I head for town, driving even faster on the way back because I'm so eager to see to the final details for my evening with Lauren. As I drive, I try to shake off that crazy thought I had earlier about raising a family in one of Blake's big new houses. Marfa is the last place on earth I'd want to raise a family, if I were going to have one.

And a family is definitely not in my plans.

*

Two hours later, I arrive at the Victorian house that Lauren has lovingly restored over the last few years. The house is a perfect reflection of her—funky, eclectic, colorful and classy. She is all those things and so much more. And when she comes to the door in a sexy red dress and the sky-high heels I requested, I'm struck dumb once again by how incredibly gorgeous she is. I remind myself of the plan for this evening, because if I could do any damned thing I wanted, I'd back her into her house and have her right here and now.

Swallowing the impulsive urge and hoping my cock gets the message to stand the fuck down, I ask if she's ready to go.

"Let me grab my purse." She turns to retrieve a bag that has red cherries on it, and I get the back view of the dress that barely covers the lower curve of her ass cheeks, which I know are bare under there.

My cock thoroughly approves of the view and pulses against the fly of the dark jeans I changed into after work. This plan of mine is going to be torture, I realize, as she returns with the purse and I notice her face is flushed the way it gets when she's turned on. I recall that detail from the night of the disaster. It's one of several facts about Lauren that I've filed away for future use. When the time is right. And the time is definitely not right tonight, or so I continue to tell myself as I help her into the Mercedes and get an eyeful of long, sexy leg and tempting inner thigh as she settles herself in the seat.

"Get your shit together," I mutter as I round the back of the car and get into the driver's seat.

"Where're we going?"

"My place, if that's okay."

"Sure."

Does she sound disappointed? What if she wanted to go out somewhere rather than have an intimate night at home alone? Hopefully, once she sees what's on the menu, she'll be happy with the plans I made for us.

This, right here, is why I don't bother with the rituals involved with dating. In all ways but one, women are a mystery to me. I never have been very good at being able to tell what they're thinking or what they want or how they really feel. So I've focused on the one area in which there are very few mysteries. I know how to fuck, and I'm never afraid to take a woman to bed, because I have little doubt she'll leave happy.

That's why I'm so determined to right this terrible wrong with Lauren. How is it possible that the only woman I've ever truly cared about was disappointed after going to bed with me? That simply won't do. No matter what happens between us in the long term, before we're finished, she'll know the truth about what I'm truly capable of when I get naked with a woman. My type-A personality refuses to settle for anything less than complete success.

We arrive at my house a short time later, and I park the Benz next to my truck on the far left side of the three-car garage, shutting the door behind us so my nosy neighbors won't see Lauren dressed to the nines getting out of my car in her come-fuck-me heels. I help her out of the car and keep a hold on her hands longer than necessary to ensure she's steady on those insane shoes. I love the feel of her soft skin and the way she holds on to me as if she knows I'll never let her fall.

I escort her inside, where I've already set the scene with music from Pandora and candles throughout the house. When I left to pick her up, I did so hoping the house wouldn't burn down in the ten minutes I was gone.

"This is nice," she says.

"I'm glad you think so. You're not disappointed that we didn't go out somewhere, are you?"

"Of course not. I'm so stinking nervous that it's probably better if we don't go out in public."

I hate to hear her say she's so nervous. "Why the nerves? It's just me and you."

"And a mountain of expectations standing between us."

"How about we ignore that mountain and focus on having a nice time tonight with zero expectations. Can we do that?"

"We can try."

I put my arms around her and bring her in close to me, while reminding my cock that he's off duty tonight. Bastard has a mind of his own, though, and the minute her sweet body presses against mine, he springs to life. "The last thing I want is for things to be weird between us."

She lays her hands on my chest and gazes up at me. "I don't want that either."

I'd have to be a stronger man than I am to resist the burning need to kiss her sweet lips. And the instant my lips connect with hers, the hum of desire that has simmered between us for as long as I can remember roars to life. That's the reason we're together tonight, why I wanted to try again with her. I've never felt for another woman what I do for Lauren. When I kiss her and hold her, that feeling multiplies exponentially.

Mindful of my agenda for this evening, I force myself to pull back from her right when the kiss is getting interesting, leaving her surprised by my sudden withdrawal. I kiss her once more. It takes every bit of willpower I can muster to keep the kiss light and undemanding. "What can I get you to drink?"

She looks up at me with those big brown eyes that are even more expressive than usual after a passionate kiss. Her swollen lips are still damp, and I work very hard to stay focused on the plan rather than the desire that claws at me.

Smiling at her befuddlement, I tap her bottom lip. "Drink?"

"Um, wine would be good. Thanks."

"Coming right up." I take her by the hand and tow her along with me to the kitchen, where I settle her on a barstool. Knowing she prefers chardonnay when she drinks wine, I bought that and the Budweiser we both like, just in case. I also have champagne for later.

As I open the bottle of wine, I can feel her watching me, and I wonder if she feels as undone by that kiss as I do. This evening is off to a promising start if the sexual tension in this room is any indication. That's exactly what I wanted—the two of us so on edge that by the time we finally get around to sealing the deal, the heat will consume us.

Thinking about spontaneously combusting inside of Lauren makes me tremble ever so slightly as I pour her glass of wine. Fortunately, she doesn't notice. I deliver the glass to her without incident and pour one for myself. "Are you hungry?"

"Starving. Something smells really good."

It had better smell good. Getting fresh lobster sent overnight from Maine to middle-of-nowhere West Texas had cost more than a thousand dollars but would be worth every penny if it makes her happy.

With a flourish, I say, "Right this way, madam."

She looks somewhat perplexed as she gets up to follow my direction into the dining room, which is set for us. I hold her chair and wait for her to get settled before returning to the kitchen to get the salads I made earlier.

After I put hers in front of her, she looks up at me. "Did you make dinner?"

"Yep."

"I thought you couldn't cook."

"I can't. Not really, but I had a little help. You'll see."

"Very interesting." She eyes me with all-new interest as she eats the salad I made myself. "I had no idea you were so domesticated."

I snort with laughter. "Don't get too excited, darlin'. Chopping lettuce is about the extent of my so-called domestication."

She continues to look at me curiously, making me wonder what she's thinking. After a long moment of silence, she says, "You went to a lot of trouble for tonight."

"Some."

"Why?"

I stare across the table at her. Is it possible that she doesn't know how much I care about her? How there's nothing I wouldn't do to make her happy? In the span of a few seconds, every minute I've spent with her in the last year flashes through my mind—our beer-and-wings nights, outings with mutual friends, helping her paint the outside of her shop a shade of yellow so bright, it hurts my eyes to look at it, and the ill-fated night when we tried to take our friendship to the next level. Does she still really wonder how I feel about her? "I... I'll tell you why after dinner."

Rattled by the emotions her question has aroused in me, I stand to clear the salad plates and return with our entrées, which I've taken right from the oven. I debated whether to get the lobsters in the shell or just the meat. In the end, I went with the meat, figuring it would be too messy and complicated to crack the shells. I followed a recipe I found online to make angel hair with a lobster cream sauce. I just hope she likes it.

"Is that *lobster*?" she asks after I put the plate in front of her.

"Sure is. Right from Maine."

"You had lobster sent here from Maine."

"Uh-huh."

"Garrett..."

"Don't let it get cold."

"But—"

"We'll talk about anything you want later. Eat your dinner."

The flash of fire in her eyes indicates she'd like to argue, but she holds her commentary and takes a bite of her meal. Then she moans.

Motherfucker. Her moan travels directly to my cock, which stands up for a better look at what's going on. The highs and lows of this evening are confusing the poor guy. First he's needed, then he's not, and now he's back but uncertain of his role in this performance.

Supporting player, I tell him. Great, now she's got me sending silent messages to my cock, messages he is clearly *not* receiving. Watching her enjoy the meal I prepared for her doesn't help the situation in my lap. Is penile whiplash a thing? If not, it should be, because I've got a bad case of it going on.

"This is so good. I can't believe you got lobster from Maine."

"Nothing but the best for you."

A rosy glow infuses her cheeks, and I go stupid in the head—the one on my shoulders. I'd give anything to know what she's thinking. *Soon enough… Stand down. Stick to the plan.* I want to tell the plan to go fuck itself and take her by the hand, drag her into my bedroom and fuck her until we're both exhausted and sated.

I down half a glass of wine in one long sip and try to eat my own dinner while it's still hot.

The landline rings, and I bite back a string of swears because the only person who ever calls that number is my mom. I want to ignore it, but I never would. "Excuse me." I get up and go into the kitchen to answer it.

"Garrett! The upstairs toilet is overflowing. I don't know what to do."

"Have you shut off the water to the toilet?"

"How do I do that again?"

Summoning the reserve of patience I save just for her and situations like this, I say, "Under the tank, there's a valve. Turn it until the water stops flowing."

"Left or right?"

"Right."

"Okay, I think I got it. Can you come look at it?"

"I can come in the morning."

"The water flooded the floor."

I close my eyes and silently count to five so I won't say something that can't be unsaid. "Get some towels and clean it up, Mom."

"Why can't you come?" she asks in the petulant tone I've become accustomed to when I'm unable to drop everything when she calls me.

"I'm in the middle of something." I pinch the top of my nose where a poorly timed headache is forming. "Where's Colby?" I ask of my twenty-two-year-old brother who moved home after finishing college in May while he looks for a job. Six months later, he's still looking, and I'm running out of patience with him, too.

"He's out with Tonya."

My brother and I are going to be having a conversation very soon about him getting a job—any job—while he figures out his career situation.

"I really think we need a plumber, Garrett. This is the third time this has happened."

"I'll send someone over to look at it."

"You're going to *pay* someone when you could do it yourself?"

"Yes, Mom, I'm going to pay someone."

"Must be nice to have all that money to burn."

The comment infuriates me. "I have to go. I'll get someone there."

"Thank you."

"Night."

As I disconnect the call, I hear her say, "Garrett—"

I have no idea what that was going to be, and I don't want to know. Withdrawing my cell from my pocket, I place a call to Blake.

"Hey, what's up?"

"I need a favor."

"Sure, whatever you need."

"Do you have a plumber you could send to my mom's? I'm tied up at the moment and can't get over there."

"I can do it myself. Honey and I are in town. I'll stop by."

"You don't have to do that."

"I don't mind."

I lean against the island in the kitchen, feeling exhausted and overwhelmed all of a sudden. "Thanks, man. I owe you one."

"Right," Blake says, laughing. "Consider it a down payment on the ten thousand favors I owe you."

"You pay me to do favors for you."

"Relax, G. I got this. Talk to you tomorrow."

"Thanks, Blake."

"Any time."

The call from my mother stresses me out the way it always does when she comes running to me for any little thing that she can't handle, which is most things. Closing my eyes, I take a minute to get myself together and recapture the mood I was building with Lauren before the interruption.

"Garrett?"

I open my eyes to find her standing in front of me, looking at me with concern.

"Is everything all right?"

CHAPTER 4

Garrett

I force a smile for her, not wanting to put a damper on our evening. "Yeah, it's all good."

She steps closer to me, placing her hands on my biceps. "Are *you* okay?"

"Sure."

"Don't lie to me. I can see right through it."

The downside to attempting to romance a woman you've known for most of your life is the inability to get away with the usual bullshit games that men and women play with each other. It's both a comfort and an added challenge to be *known* the way she knows me.

"I get frustrated with her, and then I feel like an asshole. She didn't ask to be widowed at forty-five."

"You do so much for her and your siblings. I don't know how she could be anything other than grateful to you."

"She's grateful."

Lauren raises a brow. "But?"

"I wish she didn't rely on me for every single freaking thing." In all the years since my father died, I've never said that out loud to anyone. "See? Told you I'm an asshole." I try to lighten the impact of my revealing statement with humor.

"You're the farthest thing from an asshole. You're a devoted son and brother, and your father would be incredibly proud of how well you've taken care of everyone since he died, not to mention the success you've made of his business."

Her praise warms the places inside me that have gone cold with resentment after my mother's call. "Sorry to derail our evening with this crap."

"You didn't." As she slides her hands up and down my arms, she steps closer to me, tugging lightly on my forearms until they drop to my sides. "That's better." She curls her hand around my neck and brings me down for a sweet kiss. "Now where were we before the phone rang?"

"I believe we were eating."

"I finished mine while you were on the phone. It was the best dinner I've had since the last time I had lobster." She kisses me again. "Thank you for arranging such an awesome treat."

"No problem."

"Yes, it was."

"It was worth it if it made you happy." I wonder, as I look down at her, if she feels even a fraction of what I do when we're close to each other this way. I wonder if she ever questions how it has taken us so long to get where we are right now, our bodies humming with desire and anticipation.

"Do you want to finish your dinner?"

Her question takes me out of the daze I've slipped into as I drink in the delicate features of her face. "I'm done. How about dessert?"

"As you well know, I never say no to dessert."

Grinning at her predictable remark, I kiss her again and reluctantly release her to get the chocolate cake I bought at the bakery.

"Are those from my shop?" she asks, pointing to the yellow lilies on the countertop that she has just now noticed.

"Maybe."

"How'd you pull that off without me knowing?"

"I went in after you left for the day."

"Very sneaky."

"I prefer stealthy to sneaky."

"You got my favorite color."

"Did I?" I ask with a small smile.

"You know you did. Thank you."

"You're welcome." I place the cake and the chilled champagne on the counter and get out some plates. "You want to do the honors?"

"Sure."

As she cuts the cake, I open the champagne while keeping one eye on the hem of her tight red dress as it rides up to the line between leg and cheek. I'm so focused on the view that I nearly forget to stand clear of the champagne bottle. The cork releases suddenly, launching for the ceiling as I hold the bottle over the sink.

Lauren giggles helplessly, and her laughter sparks mine.

"Smooth, huh?"

"Very."

I pour two glasses and hand one to her. "Here's to second chances."

She touches her glass to mine. "To second chances."

"Let's take dessert in the living room."

"We need to clear the dining room table."

"I'll do it later."

"Umm… Can we do it now?"

Amused by her need for order, I acquiesce. "If we must."

"We absolutely must."

Working together, we clear the table, store the leftover food and load the dishwasher. "All better?" I ask when we're done.

"All better."

I give her an indulgent smile and follow her to the sofa where we enjoy the cake and champagne.

"You went to a lot of trouble for me."

"I had fun doing it." I twirl a strand of her hair around my finger. "I like to see you smile." For so long after her marriage ended, I feared we might never see her smile again.

"Do you ever think…"

"What?"

"That this, between us, is… I don't know how to put it."

"Unexpected, even if we've both known there was something going on for a long time?"

"Yes," she says, seeming astounded by my summary. "Exactly that."

"I can only speak for myself when I say that this, between us, is something I've wanted for as long as I can remember. But the time was never right."

She frowns and looks down at her glass. "Because I married Wayne."

"Among other things. I was so overwhelmed with everything after my dad died that I wasn't exactly ready for anything serious either. I'm still not sure that's what I see for myself, even now." I fear that maybe the statement is a little *too* revealing.

"Could I ask you something?"

"Anything you want." I continue to play with her hair as we talk.

She takes a bite of cake and then feeds one to me. "If your dad hadn't died, would you have come home to Marfa after college?"

The question takes me by surprise. I've never spoken to my friends about what I'd planned to do before fate intervened. My father was the only one at home who knew what I'd planned to do after college. He and I agreed to keep the details to ourselves until I made my decision. But he died before any decisions could be made. I'm unprepared to talk to her about this. Do I tell her the truth or some version of it?

"If it's too hard for you to talk about, you don't have to," she says, apparently tuning in to my distress.

"It was a long time ago now. What does it matter?"

"If it matters to you, it matters to me."

"You're so sweet," I whisper, leaning in to kiss her. "So incredibly sweet." And sexy and smart and funny and talented. She's all those things and so much more.

"That's nice of you to say, but you didn't answer my question."

Sighing, I lean my head back on the sofa. As much as I might wish to avoid this topic, I can't start lying to her now, not with so much at stake. "I had no plans to come home to Marfa before my father died."

"What were you going to do?"

"I had applied for jobs in Austin, San Antonio and Houston."

She's silent for a long moment, so long that I wonder if I've made a huge mistake by being so honest. "That must've been a terrible disappointment on top of such a crushing loss."

Leave it to Lauren to perfectly summarize it. "Yeah," I say gruffly.

"Do you have any idea how much we all admire you for what you've done for your family since your dad died?"

"I did what anyone would do under the circumstances."

"No, Garrett, you did way more than most people would do, and you've never complained. That's so admirable. All your friends think so."

Never complained? I want to laugh at that because I feel like all I do is complain, but never to others. I keep my thoughts to myself so there's no chance of my resentment and discontent ever getting back to my mother. She didn't sign on for this situation any more than I did.

"That's nice of you to say. My dad used to tell me you have to play the hand you're dealt. That's what I've tried to do."

"You've played it very well."

Her sweetness and support present a further test of my intention to stick to the plan I put together for tonight and the rest of the week. I cup her cheek and gaze into her eyes. Then I dip my head to kiss her jawline on the way to her ear. I love that she quivers from my touch.

I put my glass on the coffee table and take hers to put it next to mine. "Come here." I reach for her and bring her onto my lap, where she can no doubt feel what her closeness has done to me. The skin on her leg is so soft against the palm of my hand. She is temptation personified, especially when I remember my request for her to be bare under her dress. Even with all my well-intentioned plans, I can't let that treasure go to waste. I look up from my study of her long, toned legs to find her watching me intently. "What're you thinking?"

"I'm actually trying to figure out what *you're* thinking," she says.

"How so?"

"This evening isn't unfolding the way I expected it to."

"What did you expect?"

"For one thing, I didn't expect lobster or champagne or flowers from my shop or chocolate cake."

"What else?" I continue to caress her leg, letting my hand wander a little higher with each careful stroke.

"I figured we'd be naked in your bed by now."

Her refreshing bluntness is an instant turn-on, even if I'm already incredibly hot for her. "Are you disappointed that we aren't?"

"No."

"Are you sure?"

"No."

I laugh at that and let my hand wander up to grasp a firm ass cheek, squeezing until she moans.

"Garrett," she says, breathless.

"Hmm?"

"What're you doing?"

"Touching you."

"Let's go in your room."

I shake my head. "Right here."

Her groan goes straight to my cock, sending an electrical current from my balls straight up my spine. I ought to be sainted for my unprecedented show of self-control. I've never before denied myself like this sexually, and I'm not entirely sure I have the willpower to follow through with my plan. She's just so fucking tempting.

I kiss her again, this time going for broke rather than teasing or flirting. Before this night is over, I want her to have no doubt that I want her badly, that I'm willing to do whatever it takes to make her see there is absolutely nothing wrong with her. Another thing my father used to tell me is that anything worth doing is worth doing right. Lauren is definitely worth doing, and I'm determined to do her right this time.

Without breaking the kiss, I ease her down to the sofa until she's flat on her back and I'm leaning over her. In this position, our kiss takes on new desperation as we strain to get as close to each other as we possibly can. Her fingers comb through my hair, holding me in place while she grinds against me, every move of her hips leaving no doubt in my mind that I could have her right here and now if I wanted. I want. I want so badly, it's become a craving, a yearning so deep that I've begun to think I'll never fully sate the need I have for her.

It would be so easy to give in, but the fear of the same thing that happened last time happening again helps me refocus on the goal for tonight—her pleasure and *only* her pleasure. I ease the spaghetti straps of her dress off her shoulders and down her arms, which makes it so she can't move her arms as I take in the rigid peaks of her bare breasts.

I want to spend a year doing nothing but worshiping Lauren's spectacular breasts, but for now, an hour will have to do. Intent on drawing out the suspense—and the pleasure—in every way possible, I begin with gentle caresses of her supple flesh, avoiding the tight tips for now. I'll come back to them later. I can tell she's surprised that I'm not in any rush, and I can tell when it dawns on her that there's not going to be any quick gratification for either of us.

A word about her spectacular breasts—they are big and perfectly shaped with light brown nipples that darken in color when she's aroused. That's something I learned the first time we did this. I also found out her breasts are incredibly sensitive, and if I handle them just right, I might be able to make her come from nothing more than intense devotion to her gorgeous breasts. Tonight, I'm out to test that hypothesis.

She squirms under me, pressing the heat of her core against my cock.

Despite my resolve, that move gets my attention and has me wishing I were less devoted to my goddamned plan. I kiss between her breasts, under them, around them, basically driving her crazy if the sounds she makes are any indication.

By the time I run my tongue over the tip of her left nipple, her eyes have glazed over and her bottom lip is swollen from being trapped between her teeth. She almost levitates off the sofa as I tongue her rigid flesh. For the longest time, that's all I do—slide my tongue back and forth while she writhes beneath me, making me as crazy as I seem to be making her.

This is what I wanted, to drive her mad and take her brain out of the equation, to make her forget that her old pal Garrett now has her tit in his mouth. I want her so hot and so bothered that she doesn't know her own name, let alone mine. As I close my teeth over her nipple and give it a gentle tug, I can see—and hear—that my goal is within reach.

She screams, and I suck hard on her nipple while pinching the other one between my fingers. I keep that up, switching back and forth from one side to the other for quite a while, so long that I lose track of time. My whole world has been reduced to Lauren's breasts and the rhythmic press of her hot pussy against my cock. If I'm driving her out of her mind, she's doing the same to me.

Drawing her left nipple into my mouth again, I run my tongue over the tip as I apply deep suction, all while pinching the right nipple harder than I have up to now.

She detonates, screaming and pulling my hair and bucking up against my cock, which is seriously pissed off with me for keeping him penned up when he could be plunging into her wet heat right now.

"Garrett," she gasps, loosening her hold on my hair ever so slightly.

I continue to suck on her nipple while gently twisting the other one.

"Please, Garrett..." She pulls on the buttons to my shirt, and one of them pings off the coffee table. Then her hands are on my chest and abdomen and pulling on my belt.

I didn't plan to let my cock out of solitary confinement tonight, but I'm unable to summon the fortitude to stop her from unbuttoning and unzipping me. The feel of her warm hand wrapped around my cock nearly does me in. But then she uses her other hand to push my pants down over my hips, and that's when I again recall that I told her to leave the underwear at home. Now there's absolutely nothing standing between me being inside her.

Time for retreat. It pains me greatly to put my hand over hers and remove it from my cock as I slide down lower on the sofa, until I'm positioned between her legs.

Her low growl of frustration makes me smile as I press kisses to her inner thigh, which trembles madly under my lips. This is going better than I expected. She's already had one orgasm, and I'm looking for another one when I push her dress up and over her hips, leaving her bare to me from the waist down. *Fucking hell...* She's so wet, her sex glistens from the moisture that's gathered there. I dive in like a starving man, licking and sucking and plunging my tongue into her. She's so incredibly sweet and responsive, rocking against me as she moans and cries out every time my tongue circles her clit.

Her grip on my hair is borderline painful, but I don't let that deter me from my goal of coaxing another orgasm from her. I push two fingers into her, stroking into her as I draw her clit into my mouth. It takes about ten seconds of that combination to send her flying once again. Success! Already this has gone two thousand percent better than the first time. As her internal muscles clamp down on my fingers, it's all I can do to hold on to my own need to come as hard as she is. But tonight is about her and only her. I bring her down slowly, sliding my fingers into her gently and running my tongue over her pulsating clit.

When I finally withdraw from her, she quivers from head to toe. As I wipe my face on the sleeve of my shirt, I notice the red dress is bunched around her belly, her nipples are tight and red from the attention I paid them, her eyes are closed, her face is flushed with color and her lips are parted. Sated Lauren is the most stunning sight I've ever laid eyes on. I press a kiss right above her pubic bone, and she jolts under me. I love how sensitive she is after she comes. I kiss each of her breasts and then find her lips in a soft, gentle kiss.

"Garrett..."

"Hmm?"

"Are we going to... Do you want to..."

"Fuck you? Hell, yes, I want to. But that's not happening tonight."

Her eyes open, and she blinks, as if to bring me into focus. "Why?"

"Because tonight is all about you and making you feel good."

"But—"

I kiss the words off her lips. "Trust me?"

"Yes, but—"

I kiss her again. "We're not on any deadline. I want to take my time and make sure we get it totally right."

"That felt totally right to me."

Smiling down at her, I say, "I'm glad to hear it."

"What about you?"

"What about me?"

"Don't you want some of what you gave me?"

So bad I can barely breathe for wanting it—and her. "Not tonight."

In the scope of one second, she transforms from satisfied to angry. She pushes me away and sits up, tugging at the bodice of her dress to cover her breasts and dragging the hem down to cover her ass. "I'd like to go home, please."

"Lauren, listen—"

She refuses to look at me. "I don't want to listen. I want to go home."

"I want to do this right, not fast, Lo. Don't be mad." I reach for her hand, but she pulls it out of my grasp. *Shit.* "Lauren, we're not leaving here until we talk about this."

"What's there to talk about? I want to have sex. You don't. I get it."

Incredulous, I say, *"Is that what you think?"* I grab her hand and press it to my still-hard cock. "Does that feel like I don't want to have sex?"

"It feels like a hard dick. How am I supposed to know what it means? If you don't want me, all you have to do is say so. There's no need to play this big game."

I take a deep breath to ensure I don't lose my shit with her, which wouldn't help anything. "I want you so bad, I burn with wanting you. I think about you and what you look like naked and how badly I fucked up that first night with you *all* the goddamned time."

She stares at me, seeming stunned by my outburst.

"This has nothing to do with me not wanting you and everything to do with not wanting to fuck up the second chance you've given me."

After a long moment, she finally blinks. "Wh-what about the second chance you've given me?"

"What're you talking about?"

"Has it ever occurred to you that things went bad between us the first time because of *me*, not you?"

"No." I say that single word as emphatically as possible. "That has never once occurred to me."

"Well, it should."

"Why do you say that?"

"Because." She swallows so hard, I can see her throat working. "I've been told before that…"

"What have you been told before?" I'm angry, and she hasn't even said it yet.

"That sex isn't my… Well, that I'm not very good at it."

In a state of total shock, I stare at her, my mouth hanging open for a second until I snap it shut. "Who told you that?" I ask through gritted teeth. I can't recall the last time I've been as fucking mad as I am right now.

She backs away from me, subtly, but I notice.

The anger recedes as fast as it flared. "Sweetheart, don't do that. Don't be afraid of me. I couldn't bear it."

"I-I'm not afraid of you."

"Come here." I reach for her and draw her into my embrace. With her head on my chest and my arms wrapped tight around her, I try to find the words I need to reassure her. "Who told you that you're not very good at sex?"

"Who do you think?"

I want to find Wayne Peterson and strangle the life out of him, but I contain that urge because rage is not the emotion she needs from me right now. "Let me assure you that couldn't be further from the truth."

"How do you know that? The only time we ever did it was a disaster. We both thought so."

"He was *wrong*." I make an effort to keep the rage out of my tone. "You're very good at it." My fingertips slide down her arm, raising goose bumps on her skin. "You know what turns me on more than anything else?"

"What?" she asks, sounding breathless again.

"When something I do makes a woman come the way you did twice tonight. That's the ultimate turn-on for me. So you see, you're actually incredibly good at it as far as I'm concerned."

"Why'd you stop, then?"

"Because I want to build the anticipation so when we finally get to the main event, there's no chance anything can go wrong. We went from being the best of friends to jumping into bed together, and it didn't work. We need a little transition time."

"Is that what tonight was? Transition time?"

"Yes. Exactly."

"Will you do something for me?"

"Anything."

"Will you clue me in on the plan so I know what to expect and what *not* to expect?"

"Yeah, I can do that."

"So what happens next?"

"Now, I take you home and we make plans for tomorrow night."

She rolls her lip between her teeth. "Do I have to go home?"

"You want to stay?"

Nodding, she says, "As long as you don't mind getting up early to meet the five a.m. flower delivery at the shop."

I groan dramatically, which makes her laugh. "I guess I can do that if it means I get to sleep with you." Grasping her hand, I get up from the sofa and tug her along with me as I lock up, shut the lights off and go into my bedroom. Alarm bells sound in my brain. Sleeping together tonight was most definitely *not* part of the plan, but I lack the fortitude to say no to her when she asks me for something. If I were thinking straight, I'd realize I ought to be far more worried about that than anything else.

"This is really nice," she says, taking in the dark wood furniture, fireplace, sitting area and artwork in my bedroom. "Are those Honey's?" she asks of the framed photographs.

"Of course. You've seen this room before."

"No, I haven't."

"I can't believe that with all the cookouts and pool parties we've had here."

"I've never been in here." With a teasing smile, she adds, "I hear there's often a line out the door to gain access."

"All lies."

"Not sure I believe that. I hear they come from all over for a roll in the hay with the Sex God."

CHAPTER 5

Garrett

I freeze in the midst of removing my shirt. "What?" My voice is hardly more than a whisper. How does *she* know *that*?

She sits on the bed and leans back on her elbows, a move that immediately reawakens my poor tortured cock. "Come on, Garrett. Don't act like you don't know what I'm talking about."

I sit next to her, keeping my back to her. "I know what you're talking about. What I want to know is how *you* know."

"People talk."

"People. What people?"

"People in this small town in which we live and work."

Fuck. Fuck. Fuck. And here I thought my tourist trade was such a well-kept secret. I turn to face her. "I want you to understand something. This, with us, is nothing like that. That was just how I killed time while I waited for you to feel better again."

"By having one-night stands with tourists?"

"Yeah, but it doesn't mean anything. It's just sex with them. It's so much more than that with you."

"You really waited for me?"

"Hell, yes, I waited. I always wanted you. I wanted to kill someone when you married that douche Wayne." God, what am I doing telling her this stuff? Words like these can't be taken back, not that I'd ever take them back, but I had plans that did not include getting this serious with her.

She sits up straight, her expression startled. "Why didn't you ever *say* anything?"

"I thought he was what you wanted, so I kept my mouth shut." Remember how I said I blame myself for her ending up with Wayne? There you have it.

Groaning, she falls back onto the bed, hands over her face. "You've got to be freaking kidding me."

I stretch out next to her and tug on one of her hands. "What do you mean?"

"Why didn't you tell me you thought about me that way?"

"When was I supposed to do that when you were spending all your time with him?"

She removes her hands from her face and looks at me with big eyes swimming with tears. "I would've dropped him like a bad habit if I'd had the slightest inkling that you were interested in me that way."

It's my turn to groan as I bury my face in my hands, frustration pumping through me. "I can't believe this. And here we thought we were such great friends."

Lauren pulls a strand of my hair playfully. "We are great friends."

I turn my face to the side so I can see her. "If that's so, how have we never talked about any of this before?"

"We were trying to preserve that great friendship. We've both been around the block enough to know that any time you go *here* with a good friend, it's a huge risk."

"I hate to think that I could've changed what happened with Wayne by saying something sooner."

"That is in no way your fault. I was young and stupid and lonely. This town... It can be a tough place to live sometimes. We're so isolated, and the local talent can be somewhat lacking. Present company excluded, of course."

"Of course," I say, smiling as I take hold of her hand and link our fingers. "We wasted so much time." Inside, I'm panicking over the serious turn this conversation has taken. We're supposed to be about one week of hot sex before I head out for greener pastures, but with every minute I spend with her, I'm getting more sucked into something significant in a place I've never wanted to be. *Fuck.*

"I prefer to think we used that time to become the people we are today, and maybe we might be ready for this now when we wouldn't have been before."

Propping myself up on one elbow, I lean in to kiss her. "I want to be very, very clear about something."

"What?" I love that breathless sound she makes whenever things get intense between us. I could very easily become addicted to that sound.

"I've wanted you for as long as I've understood what it means to want a woman." And I just keep digging a deeper hole for myself to climb out of, but I want her to know that she's sexy and desirable and lovable. The thought of her doubting herself because of that fucker Wayne makes me crazy.

"Garrett," she says on a long sigh. "I've always had the worst crush on you, even when I was with Wayne—and Blake."

Of course, I knew she'd hooked up with my friend a few times way back when, but I'd blocked that memory from my mind. "I don't like to think about that stage of our lives."

"We were bored and convenient to each other. That's all it ever was."

"Does Honey know that you slept with him?"

"Uh-huh. It was my idea for her to proposition him the night they first got together. She'd never had a decent orgasm in her life, so I suggested she take him for a ride."

"Because he knows what he's doing?" I'm unreasonably infuriated at the reminder that she once slept with my friend, even if it was years ago.

"Something like that." After a pause, she says, "That doesn't make you mad, does it?"

"No." She's turning me into a bald-faced liar. I'm fucking furious, although why I'm so furious isn't exactly clear. Could it be because I always thought of her as *mine*, even when she was married to someone else or when she'd fooled around with my friend? I'll have to chew on that disturbing thought later, when I'm alone. "That was years ago. What does it matter now?"

"Exactly."

I take a series of breaths, trying to get my emotions under control. For the first time in my life, I'm experiencing what insane jealousy feels like, and I don't like it. I don't like it one bit. I'm not sure what I want to do first—fuck the memories of Blake right out of her mind or beat the shit out of my friend for daring to put his hands on her.

"If it doesn't matter, why do you look like you want to kill someone?"

Remember what I said about being *known* by her? "It makes me crazy to think about you with any other guy." I go with the truth, because I can't hide from her.

Her hand on my face and the soft, sweet look she gives me go a long way toward easing my tension. "Every guy I've ever been with, including Blake, I wished was you."

Something inside me snaps at hearing that. I drag her into my arms and kiss her with years of pent-up desire and frustration pouring forth. Now that I'm finally allowed to show her the full extent of my desire for her, there's no holding back, no plans or self-control. There's only raw passion and desperate need. By the time I recapture my senses, I am on top of her, her legs and arms are wrapped around me, and I'm on fire for her.

"Do we really have to wait?"

Her softly spoken question permeates the fog that's overtaken my common sense. What the fuck is wrong with me? I've got the woman of my dreams in my bed asking me to make love to her, and all I can think about is what went so terribly wrong the last time we tried this and how the next time must be fucking perfect or she might always think there's something wrong with her. It takes every ounce of sanity I can muster to override the incessant throbbing in my dick to say, "I really think we should."

Her eyes close, and a long sigh escapes her swollen lips. She squirms under me, making sure I can feel the heat of her pussy against the rigid length of my cock. Message received. I begin to wonder if a man can actually die from an acute case of blue balls. Mine are probably cobalt by now. Reluctantly, I roll off her and land on my back, looking up at the ceiling and summoning the fortitude to stick with the plan.

If only we hadn't screwed this up so badly once before. If that hadn't happened, I'd be balls deep in her tight wet heat right now. The thought of that has me biting back a groan as my dick surges with excitement over the visual I've created in my own mind. *Down, boy.*

"Let me get you something to sleep in," I say as I sit up and run my fingers through my hair.

"That's okay. I prefer to sleep au naturel."

Fucking hell. Someone please just shoot me right now.

I half walk, half limp to the bathroom, where I eye the shower with lust in my heart. The only chance I have of relieving this ache and getting some sleep is if I can take the edge off. I return to the door. "I'm going to take a quick shower," I tell her.

"I'm making myself at home in your bed. Take your time."

With the vision of her naked in my bed occupying my mind, I'll be lucky if it takes ten seconds. I go through the motions of getting cleaned up, but with all the blood in my body converged in one place, it doesn't take long for my hand to end up wrapped tight around my cock. I prop my free hand against the wall of the shower and give myself over to the need for relief. I'm so primed that I immediately feel the telltale signs of impending release. Gasping, I give in to it and come harder than I have in my entire life, my whole body shaking from the explosive orgasm. I'm left breathless in the aftermath. I take greedy deep breaths and raise my face to the water to cool me off.

And even after all that, I'm still hard. Fucking awesome… I shut off the water, turn to get out of the shower, and I'm shocked to see Lauren in all her naked glory, leaning against the vanity, arms crossed under her breasts.

"I would've taken care of that for you."

*

Holy hell. I had no idea she was there, and now that I know she saw me, I'm as hard as I was before I the orgasm in the shower. Without taking my eyes off the spectacular sight of her naked body, I grab a towel and wrap it around my waist. I have no idea what to say to her audacious statement, so I go through the motions of running a comb through my hair and brushing my teeth while trying to ignore the huge tent pole under my towel. In the linen closet, I find a new toothbrush and hand it to her.

She takes it from me without comment.

I pass the toothpaste to her.

"Thanks."

We brush our teeth while making an effort to avoid eye contact in the mirror. I feel like a teenager who just got caught beating off in the shower. Even though I'm embarrassed to have been caught, I can't stop hearing her say she would've taken care of it for me. Next time, I'll let her.

I rinse the toothpaste out of my mouth and go into the walk-in closet that adjoins the bedroom. Rifling through my drawers, I find a pair of pajama pants at the bottom of a pile of gym shorts and put them on out of sheer self-preservation. If I'm intent on keeping to the bloody plan—and I'm *this* close to saying fuck the bloody plan—there's no way we can both get in bed naked.

Lauren has left the bathroom by the time I emerge from the closet. I shut off the lights and get into bed, acutely aware of her next to me.

"I'm sorry if I intruded on a private moment," she says after a long silence.

"I don't mind." With any other person on the planet, I'd be enraged, but I mean it when I say I don't mind that she saw me.

She curls up to me, her warm, soft, naked body testing my resolve like nothing else ever could. "I meant it when I said that I would've taken care of you, Garrett."

"Tonight was supposed to be about you."

"Says who?"

"Me."

"Well, there are two of us in this relationship, or whatever you want to call it, and it might be time to take this rigid plan of yours and either throw it out the window or shove it up your ass."

I laugh at her bluntness. "Is that right?"

"Uh-huh."

I realize she's now above me about a second before her lips make contact with my chest. How is it possible that one soft kiss from *this* woman makes me feel like I've been hit with a stun gun when soft kisses from other women have absolutely no effect on me whatsoever? That's another thing I'll have to think about later when I'm not under the influence of Lauren and her sexy kisses and the soft stroke of her hair over my fevered skin.

Running my fingers through that long, curly hair, I try to bring her up for a kiss, but she won't be deterred from *her* plan. *Fuck...*

Her soft kisses move from my chest to my abdomen, where she uses her tongue to trace the outline of each muscle. "Is this a six-pack or an eight-pack?"

Though I can hear the amusement in her question, I can barely breathe, let alone form a response.

"Let me count. One, two, three..." She counts to eight, tracing the outline of each abdominal muscle with the tip of her tongue. When she's done with that, she moves to the V-cut muscles that cradle my hips. I'm going to lose my shit all over again if she keeps that up. Then she pushes my pajama pants down and wraps her hand around my hard cock. I suck in a sharp deep breath. I'm on the verge of exploding, and she's barely touched me.

"I love how big you are," she whispers.

This must've been how Job felt when he was so sorely tested. Now she has me quoting the Bible. Dear *God*. She holds my cock in her tight little hand and wraps her warm lips around the head, applying just the right amount of suction as she takes me into her mouth. The orgasm in the shower might've happened a year ago rather than ten minutes. That's how fast she has me right back on the edge again.

Fucking hell, she's good at this, and *how* did she get so good at it? The thought of her doing this to Wayne fucking Peterson nearly ruins the mood, and with my dick in Lauren's mouth, I really don't want to ruin this mood. So I push all thoughts of that son of a bitch to the past where they belong and focus on the extremely pleasurable present that's unfolding before my eyes. And yes, even in the murky darkness, I can see her.

She's so hot all the time, but when she's blowing me… I don't have the words to describe how incredibly sexy it is to watch her worship my cock. And worship is the only word I can think of for the way she licks and sucks and strokes me to the point of madness.

"Lo… Lauren… *Babe*…" I give her ample warning, but she doesn't back off. If anything, she redoubles her efforts to give me the orgasm of a lifetime. I'm holding on by a fingernail when she cups my balls and squeezes—not too hard, but just right, just enough to make me blow.

She stays with me through it all, never letting up until I'm completely drained and about to beg for mercy. She releases me slowly, dragging her lips and tongue over my sensitive flesh, making me tremble like a boy who just got blown for the first time by a master. That was, most definitely, *not* part of my plan for tonight.

When I think about all the time we've wasted with other people when we could've had *this* together… My newfound high is replaced by a crushing low that reminds me of how I felt when my father died and all my choices were taken from me so suddenly. I was *this* close to my great escape and now… Now, I don't know what the fuck I'm doing. All I know is I love being with her like this. It feels right.

I cover my face with my hands and focus on breathing—and maintaining my composure, which has been thoroughly wrecked by the bewitching woman who has, one small step at a time, become the center of my world. If I let this happen with her, if I let it become about more than sex, I'm going to have to give up every other thing I want, and after waiting so long for the chance to spread my wings outside of Marfa, I'm not sure I can do that.

"Are you okay?" she asks, drawing me out of my thoughts and back into the moment with her.

"I'm far better than okay. That was amazing." I reach for her and bring her into my arms, pulling the blanket up and over us. I want to stay forever in our little cocoon, where nothing and no one can touch us, and I've never wanted anything remotely close to that with anyone else. Usually, I plan my exit strategy before the foreplay begins. But with Lauren, I feel a desperate need to keep her close, to proceed with caution, to make sure nothing can ever hurt her again—including me.

CHAPTER 6

Garrett

Unaccustomed to sharing my bed, I wake well ahead of the alarm when Lauren's warm, soft body sprawls over me. That's all it takes to make me immediately hard for her, but I don't do anything about that. I want her to sleep as long as she can. She puts in long days that begin before dawn five days a week with the flower delivery from El Paso.

As I hold her close to me, I try to remember the last time I spent an entire night with a woman. It was my senior year of college. I'd dated a girl named Marcy for about six months, and we were making some plans to stay together after graduation when my father died, and I was forced to go home to Marfa. Marcy had been to Marfa with me once, and that'd been enough for her.

When she told me she couldn't possibly move home with me, it didn't matter to me in the least. I was too busy and too grief-stricken to mourn the loss of a girlfriend who meant a lot to me until she didn't. Like my father, that relationship suffered a sudden death when circumstances intervened. I didn't have the wherewithal to care, and I've barely given her a thought in the ensuing years.

I'm not one to overanalyze myself or others, but it isn't lost on me that the part of me that was a normal young man with a girlfriend and plans for a life was stunted by the sudden loss of my father. I've never had another serious relationship since Marcy and I called it quits after my father's funeral, thus my habit of sleeping alone.

After last night, I'm trying to reconcile my own internal tug of war between wanting so badly to pursue this job opportunity in Austin—and to have more of Lauren. I've spent the better part of my adult life being torn between what I want for myself and what I've had to do for my loved ones. Now that I'm finally free and clear of family obligations and able to spread my wings, another loved one is naked and asleep in my arms.

What the hell am I doing sleeping with naked Lauren when I have one foot on the way out of the town where she's established a home and a business? A sense of panic has me carefully disengaging from her. I head for the bathroom and another shower to tend to my disobedient cock, who isn't at all happy that I left Lauren to sleep without tending to his needs first.

He and I are in the biggest fight ever right now. I need him to do what I tell him for the first time in his freaking life. He needs to stop going rogue and stick to the fucking program.

I'm all for sticking to the fucking *program if only you would stop getting in my way. I'm here to fuck. That's one of my primary purposes.*

Is my dick actually *talking* to me now? Seriously, I'm losing my ever-loving mind. As I stand under the shower, I contemplate my options.

I could speed things up, do the deed with Lauren and prove to her once and for all that there's abso-fucking-lutely nothing wrong with her.

I could continue with the original plan and draw out the suspense until I'm a hundred percent certain she's ready for the main event.

I don't have an option C.

As I contemplate my limited options, I stroke my wayward cock to yet another powerful orgasm that leaves me weak and gasping in the aftermath—two things that have only happened since I started fooling around with Lauren. Before her, an orgasm wasn't the full-body event it is when she's on my mind.

I turn my face up into the water and let it rain down upon me, wishing it could also bring some clarity to this increasingly out-of-control situation. But the water has no answers, and neither do I. I turn off the shower and open the glass door, shocked to once again find Lauren in the same spot she occupied last night.

Like then, her arms are folded under her breasts, and the sight of her splendid naked body has the rogue warrior below back on full alert. I can't win with him lately.

"A girl could get a complex from a guy who'd rather rub one out in the shower than with her."

Lauren

Waking up naked and alone in Garrett's bed, my old insecurities came rushing back to remind me that despite everything that happened last night, we still haven't had sex. And then I found him once again on a solo mission in the shower, and my insecurities went bat-shit crazy. Why would he rather do that by himself than with me when I'm already naked in his bed?

And why does he look so guilty, as if he's been caught doing something he shouldn't do rather than something that comes naturally to most guys? I don't know what to do next, and I hate that. It reminds me far too much of being married to Wayne when I never knew what to expect.

While he stands there looking stunned and speechless, I push by him and get into the shower to clean up. Who needs this shit? I've got a business to run and a life to lead, and if he'd rather get busy by himself than with me, then I have the answers I came for last night.

I'm rinsing shampoo out of my hair when I feel his arms around me. At first I'm too surprised to react, and then I'm too overwhelmed. Between the lips that are feasting on my neck, the hands that are cupping my breasts and the hard cock nestled between my cheeks, he quickly takes control of my body and mind. What was I thinking about before he showed up to scramble my brain?

Oh yeah, that it's time to cut my losses with him and move on. Except now his exceptional cock is pressing against me in an enticing rhythm while his fingers tweak my nipples, and it doesn't seem that I'm capable of doing or thinking about anything other than him.

"I wasn't in here by myself because I don't want you," he says gruffly, his breath warm against my neck. I had no idea my neck was so sensitive. "I was in here by myself because I didn't want to wake you up any earlier than necessary."

"*Garrett...*" He's driving me crazy. I want to bend over right there and let him shove that big, magnificent cock into me. I want to forget about the flower delivery and the long day ahead of me at work so I can have him every way we can think of all day long. I have never, in my five years of business ownership, thought about blowing off work for a man.

"What, darlin'?"

"You should've woken me up."

He groans loudly and continues to grind against me.

The ache between my legs is so sharp as to be painful. I try to turn to face him, but his muscular arms have me locked into place. "Easy, baby. Just like this."

I whimper from the need that has taken me over. Who knew Garrett and I would be like gas and fire when we got naked together?

You knew, my subconscious replies. *You've always known that, which is why the first time was such a huge disappointment. It wasn't supposed to have been like that with him. It was supposed to have been like* this.

As if he can tell how needy he's made me, his hand slides down my belly to slip between my legs. I'm so primed, it takes only a few strokes of his fingers in just the right place to make me come so hard, I see stars. My legs give out from under me, and only his arm tight around my body keeps me from falling.

"Are you starting to get the picture?" he asks in that sexy tone that tells me how turned on he is, too. "It's *not* you, Lauren. There is absolutely *nothing* wrong with you."

I can barely breathe, let alone speak.

"I'm so hard for you, I feel like I'm going to *burst* from wanting you."

Fuck work. Fuck the thousand dollars' worth of flowers that'll die in thirty minutes in the dry Texas heat. Fuck anything that isn't him inside me right now.

My fingers dig into the dense muscles on his forearm. "*Please*, Garrett." I add a softer but no less urgent please.

He picks me up so fast that I lose track of what's happening for a second before he carries me through the shower door and into his bedroom. "Tell me you're safe," he says as he puts me down on his bed and hovers over me, looking at me in a way that would set me on fire if I wasn't already about to lose it.

"I-I am." Is this really going to happen? Right here and now? "I've been on the pill for years."

"I am, too. I had a physical a month ago. I'd never touch you if I wasn't one thousand percent certain of that."

"I-I know." He's turned me into a stammering fool with his intensity.

Then he takes hold of his hard cock and notches it between my legs, nudging my clit, which is still tingling and throbbing from the orgasm in the shower. "This wasn't supposed to happen yet. I had a plan."

"Garrett!"

"What?"

"*Fuck your plan!*"

He releases a gasp of surprised laughter and nearly loses his composure.

I raise my hips to encourage him, and just like that, his laser focus is back.

After he teases me to the point of madness, he presses into me, and I'm immediately reminded of the last time we did this and how tight the fit had been then. It's no less so this time. The stretch of my flesh is borderline uncomfortable, which he seems to realize, retreating before he tries again. He does this over and over again, until he's fully seated inside me.

I hold on for dear life to him as he invades my body, both of us sweating from the effort it takes for him to fully enter me.

"Ah, *fuck*, Lauren," he says, sounding all growly and sexy. "You feel so fucking good. So hot and so tight and so wet." He reaches under me to grasp my ass cheeks and begins to move.

Since I've lost control of my faculties, I can do nothing but lie there and take the deep strokes that fill me to overflowing before he retreats and does it again. He's standing on the floor and has me positioned at the edge of the bed, right where he wants me so he can play my body like the god he is. The nickname, I'm discovering one deep stroke at a time, is very well deserved.

He has the lower half of my body raised off the bed, angled for the deepest possible penetration. Then he rubs against a spot inside me, a place no one has ever touched before, and I explode, screaming from the sheer force of the sensations that start in my core and roll out to every inch of the rest of me.

After that, he goes a little nuts, hammering into me with the kind of abandon I wouldn't have suspected him capable of before now. He completely lets go of the closely held control that's so much a part of who he is. I feel privileged to watch that happen, to see him unravel before me. He lays himself bare as he throws back his head and comes hard. It's so much more powerful and intense than it was when he was alone in the shower, and I feel a sense of victory at having given him that.

Oh, and the insecurities I've grappled with since the first time we tried this? They're history.

Garrett

I come down on top of her, wondering if the top of my head actually blew off or if it just feels like it did. *Holy motherfucking shit. That* was most certainly *not* part of the plan for this morning. I have never, ever, *ever* experienced anything even close to what it was like to fuck Lauren. Not even close.

My lungs ache and dots dance before my eyes, as if I've held my breath for too long. And as she snuggles me into her warm embrace, I realize I've made a mistake of epic proportions. Sex like that… It changes everything. There's no going back to just being "pals" after something like what just happened here. Fucking hell. My plan has been smashed to smithereens in fifteen unforgettable minutes.

While I lie on top of her, trying to catch my breath and make my head stop spinning, I suddenly recall an anti-drug assembly that took place during our senior year of high school. They brought in a prominent sports figure who blew his career by getting hooked on drugs. It only takes one time, he told us, to change your life forever.

Are you seeing the parallels here? As mentioned above, I like sex. I like it a lot. Up until about six months ago, I had as much of it as possible whenever I could. Now I know there's *sex* and then there's *sex with Lauren*, which are two entirely different things.

I feel her fingers comb through my hair, restoring order and making me feel loved and comforted. I'm so tempted to wallow in that feeling as well as the aftershocks that have her pussy continuing to grip my cock, which is still half hard. That alone defies belief. How can I still be hard after *that*?

"Are you okay?" she asks after a long silence.

Nodding, I say, "You?"

"Mmm-hmm."

I tell myself I've done my job here. I've restored her confidence and proved—rather definitively, if I do say so myself—that any previous issues in the bedroom were not her fault. I should get up, help her up, take another shower and get her to the shop to accept the flower delivery.

That's what I *should* do.

But my cock has other ideas. He's had one taste of Lauren's perfection, and like the junkie he is, he wants more—and he wants it right now. My semi becomes a full-blown erection in about ten seconds flat. Before my little brain takes over the show once again, I have the presence of mind to wonder if it's good for my vessels to process that much blood in the scope of seconds.

I'll worry about my vascular system later. Right now, I have far more important things to do, such as Lauren—again. I can tell I surprise her when I roll us on the big bed so I'm lying flat on the mattress looking up at her in all her befuddled glory as she sits astride me, impaled by my cock.

Her face is adorably flushed, her lips swollen and her tits exceptional. She lays her hands on my chest, almost as if she's seeking something to hold on to.

"Ride me, sweetheart." I raise my hands to her hips to guide her as she follows my direction and tries to find her rhythm. At first, she's awkward and a little hesitant, but with my enthusiastic encouragement—also known as thrusting—she gets her groove and takes us both on a wild ride. Two orgasms should have taken the edge off for me, but the tight squeeze of her pussy has me climbing long before I'm ready for this to end.

Sitting up, I wrap my arms tight around her and kiss her, sucking her tongue into my mouth. I can tell she likes that, because her internal muscles clamp down tight on my cock. Being inside her is like fucking heaven. Keeping one arm around her back, I break the kiss and cup her left breast so I can suck on the tight tip.

She screams, her head falling back, and her pussy seizing around my cock. It's unbelievable to realize the last time wasn't a one-off. For six long months, we could've been doing *this*? Not to mention the previous six *years* since I moved home to Marfa. Son of a bitch. Again, I'm left wondering how our first time could've gone so very wrong if we were capable of *this*. I'll never understand that, but this... This I understand. This I know how to do. I cup her ass in my hands and use my well-developed biceps to raise her up and down on my cock. Watching her tits bounce as she lands and hearing the sharp gasp that comes from her mouth every single time my thick base stretches her wide is like having every wet dream I've ever had come true in one absolutely fucking perfect moment.

And then she comes—hard—so hard she makes me see stars and shatters my control. I'm right there with her, making noises I've never made in my life as I unload in her again. Before I finish reeling from yet another cataclysmic finale, I start thinking about all the ways I want to have her. The first image that comes to mind is Lauren on her knees, legs spread, ass in the air, ripe for me to play with while I fuck her from behind. I wonder if she'd ever let me fuck her ass. The idea of it has me hard as a rock once again. The rogue warrior is showing me who's boss today, and I find myself in no mood to argue with him—not when it feels so damned good to let him have his way.

I have a huge workday ahead of me, meetings on top of meetings, end-of-month reports due, payroll for no fewer than ten companies to oversee, and all I can think about is how soon I can make my fantasy a reality.

"Lauren."

She raises her head off my shoulder where it landed after she came and looks me in the eye.

"I think we should call in sick."

*

In six years of running my father's business, I've never once called in sick, even when I had the flu or after I badly sprained my ankle playing a game of pickup basketball with Blake, Matt and some of our other friends. I've also never taken a real vacation. I can't be away from the business that long, so what's the point of trying to get away?

So, to say it's out of character for me to call my assistant, Tanya, and tell her I won't be in today is putting it mildly. I render poor Tanya speechless.

"You're doing *what?*" she asks in the Texas twang that adds extra syllables to every word. Across the room, Lauren is on the phone with the high school student she employs part time, asking her to run by the shop to bring in the flowers and put them in the fridge before she goes to school.

"Oh, and put a note in the window that we'll be closed today," Lauren adds.

I tune in to her explaining that she's too sick to come to work and nearly forget that Tanya asked me something.

"Garrett! What's *wrong* with you?"

I try to think of something, but my mind has been wiped clean of any thoughts that don't involve being inside Lauren's delectable body. "I…"

"Do you need me to come over there?"

"No! Definitely not. Stomach flu. It's *bad*."

"Ohhh, okay. Poor baby. That's the worst. I'll reschedule your day. Will you be able to check your email later to approve the payroll?"

With her call taken care of and after a trip to the bathroom to clean up, Lauren crawls across the bed and wraps herself around me, her breasts flat against my back.

"Garrett?"

"What's that?"

"Payroll."

"Oh, right, yes. I'll look at it this afternoon."

Lauren, that sexy witch, reaches around me and begins stroking the rogue warrior, who's back on full alert, prepared to do battle again at a moment's notice. He's indefatigable. I'll give him that. Then she bites my earlobe, and I jolt.

"Do you need anything?" Tanya asks. "Soup or ginger ale or crackers?"

"No, thanks," I say, clearing the gruffness from my throat. "I'm good." So, so, *so* good.

"Check in with me later. I've never had to get through a day without you here. I'm not sure I can handle it."

"Do what you can and put the rest on hold until tomorrow." My staff won't run my business into the ground if I take one day off, will they? I experience a twinge of anxiety that's quickly trumped by lust as Lauren enthusiastically pumps my cock with her soft little hand. "I've got to go."

"Feel better."

I feel so good, better than I have in ages, as long as I don't think about what this means or how it impacts the plans I've made for myself. "Thanks." I toss my phone aside and grab hold of Lauren's hand to stop her from finishing me off before I can live out that fantasy I had earlier.

"On your hands and knees," I tell her. "Now." As I'm looking at her over my shoulder, I can see her eyes widen with shock and then desire so blatant it makes me groan in anticipation.

She does as directed, but I notice her legs are trembling, so I stuff a pillow under her hips to provide support for what's about to happen here.

"Are you comfortable?"

"Uh-huh." Fisting the sheet, she holds on tight.

I start at her calves, running my hands up the backs of her legs, taking my time to draw out the anticipation for both of us. Her legs are finely muscled and her ass a work of art, both a testament to the time she spends at the gym. As someone who works out as much as I do, I appreciate others who put in the time to keep fit, not to mention I appreciate benefitting from the perfection that is Lauren's sweet body.

I'm practically drooling from the sight of her spread open for me to do whatever I want to her. But then I remember Wayne and what he put her through. She's never confirmed that his attack involved sexual assault, and I've never asked. But I suspect it did.

"Lo..."

"Hmm?"

"You'd tell me if something I did scared you or brought back bad memories, wouldn't you?"

She shoots me a look over her shoulder. "Yeah."

"Are we okay here?"

Nodding, she gifts me with a smile that sparks a curious tingling sensation in my chest, not unlike gas or heartburn or something in that family. I have no idea what to call this sensation, but it also comes with a feeling of contentment that has eluded me for most of my adult life.

But with the all-you-can-eat Lauren buffet spread out before me, I can't take the time to contemplate contentment—or gas. I've got better things to do. Raising my hands to her supple ass, I spread her cheeks wide open, drawing a sharp gasp from her. For a minute, I simply revel in the sight of her pretty pink flesh, moist with desire for me. The most incredible proprietary feeling overtakes me. She is *mine*. I would kill anyone who hurt her and not give a thought to the consequences.

I'm so fucked, but I'll worry about that later. Right now, I have much better things to do than think about consequences. Holding her open, I dive into her sweetness, licking from front to back and everywhere in between.

She goes wild, pressing her ass against my face with the kind of desperation I certainly understand. I'm already so hard—again—that I worry that my skin will burst from trying to contain the desire that pumps through me like an extra heartbeat. This is absolute madness, and I can't get enough of her.

I go at her until I can tell she's on the verge of release, and then I push inside her again, triggering her orgasm. Biting my lip—hard—I try to hold off until I can get her there again and somehow manage to hang on to my control, but just barely. That, too, is unprecedented. Usually after the edge is taken off the first time, I'm like a fucking machine, but not with Lauren.

Grasping her hips, I pump into her, loving her gasps and moans and the way she clings to the comforter as if it's a life ring in a wild sea. I love the way her ass jiggles ever so slightly every time I bottom out, and I absolutely adore the way her tight pussy clamps around my cock. I could do this all fucking day and never get tired of the way it feels to be inside her. In fact, it might be the very best feeling I've ever experienced.

I soak my fingers in her slickness and press them against her anus.

She bucks from the unexpected pressure, but I'm ready for her with my other arm tight around her waist.

"Let me in, sweetheart."

She moans and presses back against my fingers, her flesh yielding to allow me in. Fucking hell… She's so hot and so tight, more so now with my fingers in her ass.

Then she implodes. There's no other word to describe the orgasm that blasts through her. She clamps down on my cock and fingers, her release triggering mine, because there's no way I can hold back with her muscles squeezing me so tightly. My mind goes completely blank as I unload in her. There're no worries about my company, my family, my future or anything else. I have only the capacity to think about her and this and us. Being with her this way is like taking a vacation from my life without ever leaving my own bed.

CHAPTER 7

Garrett

I withdraw from her slowly and carefully, making her groan from the pressure as I remove my fingers. On shaky legs, I go into the bathroom to wash up and bring back a warm washcloth to tend to her. She's facedown on my bed, and my gaze is immediately drawn to the red finger marks I've left on her hips. She's going to have bruises because of me, and I feel bad about that.

"Turn over and let me see your gorgeous face."

"I can't move."

"Let me help." I roll her over and brush the hair back from her face. "Hi there."

She looks away. "Hi."

"What's wrong?"

"Nothing."

"Then why can't you look at me?"

"I'm embarrassed."

"Because of what we did?"

She bites her lip and nods.

"Look at me."

"I can't."

Laughing softly, I cajole her with my fingers caressing her face. "Please?"

Slowly, she brings her gaze to meet mine, her cheeks flushing in an adorably sweet blush.

"There you are. Why are you embarrassed by what we did?"

"I... I haven't done *that* before."

"Which part? The doggie or the anal?"

And I've lost her again. Her eyes are back on the far wall of my bedroom rather than on me. "*Lauren,*" I say in a singsong voice. "Come on, talk to me." I kiss the delicious column of her neck and bite down on her earlobe.

She jolts, which makes her tits bounce, and I can't believe the stirring that occurs in my groin. This can't be healthy, and yet it feels like the healthiest thing I've done for myself in years. Grasping her leg, I encourage her to open to me so I can clean her up. She allows it, but her blush deepens, and I'm intensely charmed by her embarrassment.

But I can't let her pull away from me now. That simply isn't going to happen. After I finish tending to her, I crawl into bed with her and draw her into my embrace, settling her head on my chest. "I'm not making you look at me, so now you can tell me what part of that embarrassed you."

"It wasn't what we did so much as the intensity. That was... I haven't... Not like that."

"Me either, sweetheart." As we talk, I run my fingers through her hair. "It's never been like that for me."

"Are you freaked out, too?"

"Little bit."

"That makes me feel better."

"Will you do something for me?"

"After the most spectacular orgasms of my life, you could pretty much ask me for anything."

I grunt out a laugh at her bluntness. "Will you talk to me about what you're thinking and feeling? We both said that our friendship is the most important thing, and to protect that, we have to talk it out."

"I'm not used to that. Most of the guys I've been with are more about the wham, bam, thank you, ma'am, than they are about communicating."

"I've been guilty of that myself in the past, but this is too important to both of us to get away with that this time. You know?"

"Yeah," she says with a deep sigh. "I know."

"So what part embarrassed you? The doggie or the anal?" I really want—and need—the answer to that question.

"The, um… The anal. I haven't done anything there before."

"Did you like it?"

"Ah, yeah… You couldn't tell?"

"I could tell," I reply smugly, earning an elbow to the ribs that makes me gasp with laughter.

"It's not funny. I'm a good girl. I don't do anal."

Her prim tone only makes me laugh harder. "Hate to be the one to break it to you, darlin', but you just did anal."

"If you keep laughing at me, that'll be the last time I ever do it."

I somehow manage to curb my laughter, but it isn't easy. She's so damned cute when she tries to be proper shortly after clawing at my comforter while I fucked her and fingered her ass. I can't even think about the vision of her bent before me, my cock stretching her pussy and my fingers in her ass. I force the visual from my mind because I know she needs a break in the action after the morning we've already put in.

"Does that mean you'd do it again?" I ask after a period of silence.

"Maybe."

"Would you consider more than just my fingers?"

She groans, and the sound goes straight to my balls, probably because her leg is pressed up against them. "You'd cripple me with this thing." For emphasis, she squeezes my cock, and I nearly launch off the bed.

"A little warning before you grab hold of my stick shift would be nice."

She loses it laughing, and I find myself falling, as if I've stepped off a cliff into the unknown. The sensation is so dizzying that it takes my breath away.

"And P.S.," I say, trying to shake off the odd feeling, "I wouldn't cripple you. I bet you'd love it so much you'd be begging me to fuck your ass again."

"I'd take that bet if it didn't mean having to take *this*…" She squeezes me again. "*There*." Before I can formulate the proper response, she continues. "Although if Honey can do it with Blake and his massive *thing* without being crippled, I suppose anything is possible."

I choke on my own spit. That was way more information than I ever wanted about our friends, especially the part about Blake's "massive thing."

"You can't ever let on that I told you that!"

I'm still coughing rather inelegantly, but I hold up my hand to stop her from freaking out. "Your secret is safe with me."

"She would kill me for blurting that out."

"I can't believe you guys talk about stuff like that."

"Of course we do," she says, as if that's the most ridiculous thing I've ever said to her, and I've said a lot of ridiculous things to her over the years. "Like you guys don't talk, too."

"Um, for the record, Blake and I have never talked about whether he and his wife do anal. In fact, we've never talked about anything they do in the bedroom."

"Like… nothing?"

"Nothing."

"Wow, that's kinda surprising. I thought you guys talked about it the way we do."

"Nope, and that's just one of many ways me and my boys are maligned." I tweak her nose. "It's you *girls* who do all the kissing and telling, not us."

"Whatever you say, stud." Her stomach lets out a loud growl that has her blushing once again. "That was ladylike."

"My lady is hungry. I must feed her so I can ravish her some more. Let me up, woman." I kiss her on my way out of bed to see to breakfast. We're both going to need some fuel to get through this day.

*

By five o'clock that afternoon, we're exhausted and sated and thoroughly and completely fucked in more ways than one. I'm addicted to everything about having sex with Lauren. That one taste led to another and another and another. I've never gorged on any woman the way I have on her today.

And this daylong fuckfest is nowhere near enough. That's the part that has me freaked out the most. With her warm and soft and curled up in my arms, I still want her, which is just another in a long line of surprises. Usually, I'm a one-and-done kind of guy. At times, I've thought that I have sexual ADD because women don't hold my attention. I enjoy them, I treat them right while we're together, and then I move on. I rarely ever give them another thought after we've both gotten what we wanted from a liaison.

This, with Lauren, is completely different, mostly because I'm more intrigued by her after we had sex than I was before. And that is most definitely a first. I know that might make me sound like a dick, but I've always been respectful and forthright in my dealings with women. I let them know what I want—and what I don't. No one is ever hurt or left wondering what happened with me. That's not how I roll.

Now, I'm worried about doing actual damage to a woman for the first time in my life. What will Lauren think when she finds out I'm making plans to leave town? Will she be disappointed or hurt or worse? The possibility of that gnaws at me and makes me feel anxious when I should be as relaxed as I've been in years.

Lauren and I are watching a movie in my bed because she's legitimately afraid she won't be able to walk tomorrow if we don't quit while we're ahead. The chick flick she chose doesn't hold my interest and gives me far too much time to think about what the hell I'm going to do about the plans I've been making for myself now that I've experienced the exquisite pleasure of making love to Lauren.

When I checked my email earlier to approve the payroll the office sent over, I also read an email from my headhunter, who forwarded a gushing message from the company I'm meeting with on Saturday about how excited they are to have me in to talk. They're putting me up in a suite at the Four Seasons and told me to bring my wife or girlfriend if I'd like. They even mentioned a spa at the hotel that would be made available to my guest. Lauren would love that.

As I stroke her arm absently, I start to ask if she wants to come, but something stops me from saying the words that are on the tip of my tongue. Instead, something else entirely comes out. "Have we proven beyond a reasonable doubt today that there is nothing wrong with you when it comes to sex?"

"I believe we have."

"So no more thinking there's anything about you that isn't perfect, you hear me?"

"I hear you." She looks up at me, her eyes soft with emotion. "Thank you, Garrett."

"It was a tough job, but someone had to do it."

She laughs, as I hoped she would, and returns her attention to the movie.

I nearly launch out of bed when I hear the alarm system chime to indicate someone has come into the house. And since only one other person has the key to my house, I know exactly who it is. I hastily pull on a pair of sweats and tell Lauren to stay put.

"Who is it?" she asks.

"My mother."

"Ohhh."

"I'll be right back." I leave the bedroom, closing the door behind me and go into the kitchen, where my mother is stirring a pot on the stove.

"There you are. Tanya called to tell me you've got the stomach bug. I brought you chicken soup and Ritz crackers. Remember how much you loved them when you were little? You'd go through a stack a day. And there's ginger ale in the fridge and strawberry Jell-O. All your favorites."

Though I want to be annoyed by her—and at Tanya, for Christ's sake—for barging into my house without calling first, how can I be when she just wants to take care of me? "Thanks, Mom."

"Are you feeling better?" She takes a close look at me and reaches up to feel my forehead. "You're a little warm. Have you taken something for the fever?"

"I'm much better, but you shouldn't breathe the air around here just in case it's contagious. You don't want to get sick or take it home to Colby or Sierra."

"They're bulletproof when it comes to germs. They never get sick, and neither do I. Do you want me to sit with you while you eat?"

"You don't have to. I'm not really ready for food yet."

"My poor baby. Always taking care of everyone else. I was glad to have the opportunity to do something for you for a change." She reaches up to smooth my hair and pats my cheek.

A word about my mom here—she's drop-dead gorgeous and always has been. She has long dark hair and flawless brown skin that comes right from her mother, who was Mexican. My sisters, Colby and I share her coloring, while Tommy favors our dad, who was English and Scottish. To my knowledge, my mom hasn't so much as talked to another man since my father died, let alone dated. Her dark brown eyes are soft with maternal concern as she looks me over. "What's that on your neck?"

"What?"

She points to the spot. "That."

I go to the microwave to check my reflection in the glass door. Son of a fucking bitch. I have a bite mark on my neck. "I don't know." I feel like a teenager who just got busted by his mother for having a hickey.

She folds her arms and sizes me up. After raising four children, she's nobody's fool. "Who is she?"

"Mom..."

"Are you really sick or faking it?"

Immediately flustered by the way she homes in on the truth of the matter, I stick to my story. "I'm sick. And I'm a grown man, and this is my house. I don't have to answer to you."

"Watch your mouth with me, Garrett McKinley."

"I don't mean any disrespect. You know that. But I'm not up for a grilling about my personal life. Not tonight." My emotions are already all over the place after the day I've spent with Lauren. I don't have the fortitude to deal with my mother's questions on top of that.

"Fair enough."

I kiss her cheek. "Thank you for the soup and everything."

"You're welcome."

As I walk her to the door, I ask, "Did Blake fix the toilet?"

"He did. He's such a sweet boy, and Honey is the most adorable pregnant woman I've ever seen."

"She really is cute."

"I'll be surprised if she makes it past the weekend."

"They're so ready for that baby to get here."

At the door, my mom stops and turns to me, placing a hand on my chest as she looks up at me. "That's all I want for you. What they have. At some point, you're going to want to settle down and have a family of your own, Garrett."

No, I want to say, that's about the last thing I want after being responsible for your family for the last six years. But I don't say that. I'd never say that to her. "I hear you, Mom. When the time is right."

She goes up on tiptoes to kiss me. "Take care, honey."

"Thanks again."

For a few minutes after she leaves, I keep my forehead pressed to the back of the door, trying to collect my thoughts so I can go back to Lauren with my head screwed on straight.

"Everything all right?" Lauren asks from the doorway to my bedroom.

I turn to find her wearing only my discarded dress shirt buttoned once in the middle of her breasts. Her long, toned legs are on full display, along with her bare pussy, and my mouth waters at the sight of her.

"Garrett?"

"Yeah, I'm fine."

"What did your mom want?"

"She brought me chicken soup and Ritz crackers."

"Remember how you used to eat them nonstop in high school?"

Her question is a reminder of how far back we go, how well we know each other, how much is at stake. "I remember—and so does she. You want some soup?"

"I wouldn't say no to that."

I scoop the hearty soup into bowls and take a sleeve of crackers from the box to share with Lauren.

"Oh my God, this is good," Lauren says.

My mom is an amazing cook, and almost everything she makes, even chicken soup, bears a hint of her mother's native Mexico. I've yet to have better Tex-Mex anywhere than what we got at home growing up.

"She noticed the hickey you gave me."

Lauren's spoon freezes halfway to her mouth. "What hickey?"

I point to my neck.

She gasps. "Oh crap. What did she say?"

"She asked me who'd been biting my neck, so I told her that sweet little Lauren Davies grew up to be a hellcat in bed."

"*Youdidnotsaythat.*" The words come out in one long breath.

I laugh my ass off at the look of horror on her face. "No, I didn't say that."

"Damn it, Garrett! That's not funny!"

"Yes, it really is." I can't stop laughing at her indignation.

"You know how much I've always loved your mom. She was so good to me when we were younger and my mom was… well, not around or bombed out of her mind. She even took me prom dress shopping and paid for my dress. Do you remember that?"

"Yeah, I do." The reminder of Lauren growing up with a mother who was a violent alcoholic sobers me. We all believe she married Wayne more to escape the ongoing drama with her mother than because she loved him. I've wondered so many times what might've been different if I'd stepped up for her in some way before he did. But I was in college by the time that went down and under the misguided assumption that there'd be a chance for us later.

By the time I came home, she'd been married a year already, and the handwriting was on the wall that she'd traded one awful situation for another.

We finish eating in silence and do the dishes together because I know she won't let them sit in the sink overnight the way I would have. When we're done, I turn to her and tuck a stray strand of hair behind her ear before tracing the fragile shell of her ear, my finger bumping over the array of studs that line her ear. She is so strikingly beautiful in a fragile sort of way that keeps me on guard against things that could ever hurt her.

"What do you want to do now?" I ask her, my hands on her shoulders.

"I should probably go home before I outstay my welcome."

I'm stunned that she would worry about such a thing, and I'm suddenly desperate to keep her from leaving. "That's not possible."

"I came for dinner last night and never left," she says, smiling up at me.

"Do you see me complaining?" I drop my hands to her waist and draw her into my embrace. I don't even care that she can feel that I'm hard for her again. "Stay with me tonight. I'll get you to the shop for the flower delivery in the morning." I kiss her forehead. "I promise."

"Are you sure you aren't tired of me?"

I rub my hard cock against her soft belly. "I'm very sure."

CHAPTER 8

Lauren

It's still dark when the alarm goes off in the morning. I wake disoriented and uncertain of where I am until I feel Garrett's arm around me and his warm naked body pressed up against my back. None of the anxiety that usually plagues me at night showed up while I was in his bed, allowing me to sleep better than I have in a long time.

I feel bad that I have to drag him out of his warm bed so early, but I can't ask Megan to do the flower pickup two days in a row. I try to ease my way out of his embrace to go grab a quick shower, but he tightens his hold on me.

"Not yet," he mutters in a gruff, sleepy voice.

"I have to get to the shop. Don't forget. You promised."

He groans and lets me go, rubbing his hands over his face before he jumps out of bed with more energy than he should have at this ungodly hour. The early wakeups are the only part of owning Bloomsbury that I don't love. Otherwise, the shop has been one of the best things I've ever done. About four years ago, I used the small bequest from my late grandmother to pay the first six months of rent on the storefront with the idea that if the shop didn't take off, all I'd be out was six months of rent and a lot of hard work.

The shop took off in ways I never could've expected, with many of the local hotels and restaurants placing daily orders that keep me going, in addition to the cash cows of Valentine's Day, Easter, weddings, funerals, proms and other events that provide a steady flow of business through my sweet little shop.

I nearly lost everything last year when a water main broke on Highland, flooding out the street and most of the businesses. Only the quick action of Blake and Garrett and my other friends saved my business from disaster. I can't even think about that day without feeling sick over what almost happened. Thank God for good friends.

"I'm going to grab a quick shower," I tell him.

"Mind if I join you?"

"Of course not." After what we did all day yesterday and then again last night after we went to bed, I'm surprised I can still walk today. Then he suggests we shower together, and my body lights up with desire, as if I haven't had more sex in the last twenty-four hours than I had in the entire time I was married to Wayne.

Ugh, why would I ever compare Garrett to him in any way? There is, simply, no comparison.

I follow him into the shower and put my arms around him from behind, resting my face against his back.

He stiffens with surprise but then relaxes a bit.

"Thank you." The two little words seem so inadequate in light of the boost my self-confidence has received thanks to him.

"It most definitely was my pleasure to service you," he teases as he covers the hands I've placed on his abdomen with his own hands. "We can't have you walking around thinking that you're anything other than perfect and sexy and desirable and wonderful." He turns to face me, and I'm caught off guard by the intense way he looks at me. His hands frame my face, forcing me to gaze up at him, not that it's a hardship. He's even more handsome in the morning, with his jaw covered in dark stubble and his hair standing on end. "Don't ever let anyone make you feel like you're anything less than amazing, Lo."

"I'll try not to." I wonder if he's giving me this advice before we go back to being just friends, or if there will be more of what we've shared while locked away in his home together. Do I want more than just friendship with him? I think maybe I do, but I'm so confused right now. I have no idea what he wants, and I can't bring myself to ask him. I need Honey. She'll know what I should do.

He washes my hair, and then I return the favor. Then he washes me with the body wash that smells like him. He's very thorough, leaving no part of me untouched. By the time he's finished, I'm panting with desire for more of him, basically answering my own question.

Apparently, he feels the same way, because he lifts me into his arms and presses my back against the cool shower wall.

"Are you too sore for more?" he asks in that gruff, sexy tone that's quickly become one of my favorite new discoveries about him.

"Probably."

He presses his hard cock against my core, carefully but intently, letting me know what he wants as much as I do.

"But I'm willing to try if you are." I'm going to be late for the flowers, and I can't bring myself to care.

"I'm more than willing," he says with a dirty grin that makes me laugh.

God, he's so freaking sexy when he's unshaven and disheveled from sleep. I realize I've never seen him this way. He's always so put together, so professional and well groomed. I love that I'm getting to see this side of him.

He enters me slowly and carefully.

I'm not going to lie. It hurts. A lot. So I cling to him and grit my teeth through the pain, which subsides after a few minutes of patience on his part. By the time he's fully seated inside me, I'm already on the verge of explosive release.

He grips my ass and begins to retreat before diving back in and triggering an orgasm that rips through me like a tsunami, leaving no part of me unaffected by the power of it.

"Fucking hell," he mutters, his lips against my neck setting off aftershocks. "That was so hot."

As he picks up the pace, I realize I'm the only one who came. Dear God, he's going to cripple me, but what a way to go. With every deep thrust, he ruins me for all other men. I'm quite convinced that no one else could make me feel as safe and as treasured and as sexy as Garrett does. I want more of him. I want so much more. I want to feel this way every day for the rest of my life. I want to be with him as friends and lovers and life partners. I want everything.

The realizations, coming one on top of the other, have me reeling from the emotional wallop.

Garrett continues to fuck me with the kind of abandon I suspect he rarely allows himself. "I wish we could do this all day again today," he says harshly, his fingers digging into the dense flesh of my ass as he has his wicked way with me.

Pinned against the wall, I'm absolutely powerless to do anything but take every deep stroke, and I love being powerless with him. Knowing he would do anything for me before we ever stepped foot into a bedroom together makes it possible for me to let go, too, to give myself completely to him.

"Ah, God, *Lauren…*" His entire body goes taut in the seconds before he comes deep inside me.

I wrap my arms around his neck and hold on for dear life to the man who has been my rock for such a long time. Somehow I have to find a way to tell him that I want this to be the beginning of the next phase for us—the phase in which we live happily ever after together.

As his body trembles in the aftermath of his release, I feel confident that he wants the same things I do. After this incredible time together, I can't imagine either of us with anyone else. I'm going to talk it out with Honey, and then tonight, I'll talk it out with him. This has to be a new beginning for us, not the end.

Garrett

I didn't plan to make love to her again in the shower, but we know what's become of my plans since the rogue warrior took over my program, which has been blown to smithereens. Shredded. Dismantled. Absolutely nothing has gone according to my carefully crafted plan. But the outcome has exceeded my wildest expectations.

Lauren now knows without a shadow of a doubt that there's nothing wrong with her performance in the bedroom. In fact, if her performance had been any more outstanding, I wouldn't be able to walk today. As it is, I'll probably have a slight limp from the ache in my groin. I'll never forget the image of her straddling my face last night and then bending forward to suck my cock while I licked her pussy. It was fucking amazing, but if I allow myself to think about that, I'll be hard again in no time.

I *have* to go to work today. That's nonnegotiable. With that in mind, I take the time to shave in the shower while Lauren goes to get dressed. She returns to the bathroom to brush her hair, and with my eyes drawn to her rather than the mirror, I slice my chin wide open. "*Fuck!*"

"What?"

"Cut myself shaving."

"Ouch. Are you okay?"

"Yeah." But the bleeding is profuse, and the metaphor isn't lost on me—take your eye off the game and end up bleeding. When I step out of the shower, Lauren is there with first aid supplies she must've unearthed from the bathroom closet. She presses gauze to my chin and applies pressure until the bleeding slows. Then she dabs antibiotic ointment on the cut.

As she works, she rolls her bottom lip between her teeth and is intent on her task. "I think you're going to live," she says, smiling up at me.

I'm completely dazzled by the smile, by the pleasure of having her here with me as I start my day, by the way she took care of me and... She's lovely to look at. So fucking lovely.

"Garrett? Why're you staring at me?"

"You're very pretty in the morning. All the time, but I like how you look in the morning."

She wrinkles her nose. "I haven't even put on mascara yet."

"You don't need it." I kiss her nose and go into my closet, located off the bathroom, to get dressed in my usual work uniform of dress pants and a starched shirt. Most days, I don't bother with a tie, but with back-to-back client meetings today, I put on a tie.

When I emerge, Lauren is seated on the countertop, legs crossed, doing something with a nail file. My gaze runs the length of her leg, from the tips of her coral-colored toes to the firm, toned calves to the hem of the dress she wore for our dinner the other night, which lands above her knee. Remembering she left the panties at home, I have to look away or I'll be sidetracked once again.

"Ready?"

"Uh-huh." She jumps down from the counter and slides her feet into those sexy fuck-me heels.

We leave my house and drive into town. Rather than taking her home, I head for her shop on Highland.

"Where're we going?"

"To the shop. I thought I could help you with the flowers before I take you home."

"Oh, thanks, but you don't have to do that."

"I don't mind." I park behind the shop, and we work together to bring in the buckets of flowers that have been left in the alley behind the store. It's dark and desolate. "I'm not sure how I feel about you doing this by yourself every morning."

"What? Why?"

"It's not safe."

"Sure it is. I never feel unsafe here. It's my happy place."

I bite my tongue, because I certainly don't want to plant fear in her mind, but I make a note to get her some mace or pepper spray so she can defend herself if need be. The thought of being more than six hours away in Austin and something happening to her makes me feel queasy. I'll ensure she's safe before I go.

We stash the buckets of flowers in the cooler and lock up the shop. On the way to her house, we pass the local doughnut shop, which is one of the few businesses open at this hour.

I pull into the drive-through.

"What're you up to?" she asks, smiling.

"Breakfast. What do you feel like?"

"If we're splurging, I'll have a cinnamon sugar."

I order four doughnuts and two coffees with cream, handing the bag and beverage carrier to her.

"My mouth is officially watering," she says, sniffing the air in the car that is now full of the scent of hot doughnuts.

I pull into her driveway a few minutes later, take the coffee from her and follow her into the house, planning to eat and head to work. No matter how delicious Lauren might be, I can't touch her again or I'm apt to lose another day of work. That's how tempting she is to me.

We sit at the bar in her kitchen to eat our doughnuts and drink our coffee.

"So, so, so good," she says, sighing. "I allow myself one per month or I'd be nine hundred pounds."

I'm transfixed by the sight of sugar on her lips and the blissed-out expression on her face. Without thinking about what I'm doing, I lean in to kiss those sugary lips. She's so damned sweet, and then she smiles at me, and I again experience that curious feeling inside that has me rubbing the aching spot on my chest.

I link my fingers with hers. "I have to get to work."

"I do, too." But she doesn't let go of my hand.

I give a halfhearted tug, and she tightens her grip. Smiling, I say, "I had the best time."

"I did, too. Thank you for all of it—the lobster, the champagne, the orgasms, the badly needed boost to my self-confidence."

"You're absolutely perfect. Don't you dare ever think otherwise."

"I'll try not to." She looks up at me, madly vulnerable. "Will I see you later?"

"I… I'm not sure. I need to hit the gym after work."

"You might see me there."

That wouldn't be unusual. We often work out together at the end of the workday. What *would* be unusual is being there together under our new status as friends who have fucked. A lot.

I give her a soft, lingering kiss and draw back from her. Disengaging is for the best, or so I tell myself. "Have a good day."

"You, too."

As I drive the short distance to my office, the feeling that I've left something important behind overwhelms me. The feeling stays with me throughout my morning meetings, in which I'm so distracted that, more than once, I lose the thread of conversation and have to scramble to catch up before the clients realize I've checked out.

The feeling intensifies when I take a call from my potential employer in Austin who is eager to finalize the plans for Saturday's meeting. Marilyn, the CEO's executive assistant, walks me through the schedule for the day.

"Will you be bringing a guest?" she asks.

"I…" Will I be bringing a guest? I need to think about this. "Could I let you know that tomorrow?"

"Of course. Not a problem. I've sent you the confirmation for your suite at the Four Seasons. You're booked for Friday and Saturday nights, but please let me know if you'd like to add Sunday, at our expense, of course."

"That's very nice of you, thank you. I'll let you know."

"Perfect. We're so looking forward to meeting you. Mr. Dutton is thrilled that you've agreed to come in."

I rub at my chest where that ache I experienced earlier has intensified. I'm really doing this. I'm actually making plans to leave Marfa and pick up my life where it left off six long years ago. "Tell him I'm looking forward to meeting him, and please pass along my thanks for the VIP treatment."

"Our pleasure. The driver will meet you at the hotel on Saturday morning at nine."

"I'll be ready."

Long after I end the call, I sit behind my desk, staring off into space, my brain working overtime trying to process everything that's happened in the last week. I went from years of simmer with Lauren to full-on boil. I've gone from working with a headhunter for a year to an honest-to-goodness hot lead on the kind of job I've always wanted.

The convergence of those two things has me more mixed up than I've been in years, since my father died and I was forced to abandon my own plans so I could pick up the baton for my family.

A knock on the door drags me out of the contemplation, but I continue to rub at the ache in my chest, wondering if I have heartburn or possibly something worse. With my father dropping dead of a heart attack at fifty-two, my thoughts linger on the second possibility, which of course totally freaks me out.

"Yeah, come in," I call to the person who knocked.

My second-in-command, Dennis, comes in. "Hey, boss, you feeling better today?"

"Yeah, much. What's up?"

He catches me up on a few things I missed yesterday and, as usual, impresses me with his attention to detail and his concern about pleasing our clients. If the job in Austin materializes, I decide to give him a big raise and hire him to manage my firm in Marfa.

It's all falling into place, just the way I always hoped it would. So why the hell does my chest ache so badly?

Lauren

Honey saves me the trip by dropping into the shop with a coffee for me and a soy latte for herself that she complains about the entire time we're enjoying our beverages in my workroom.

"I can't wait to be able to mainline caffeine again." She puts her swollen feet up on one of the empty chairs at the table where I eat lunch just about every day. "Maybe then I won't feel like I'm wading through quicksand."

"Um, you do know that you can't drink caffeine when you're breastfeeding, right?"

"Shut your filthy mouth. I know!"

I laugh at her indignant response.

"Screw caffeine. You have a lot of explaining to do, missy. Starting with the fact that you went to dinner at Garrett's two nights ago and didn't resurface until this morning."

"Did I do that?" My face goes hot with embarrassment, which is silly, really. This is Honey, for crying out loud. What do I have to be embarrassed about with her? We tell each other everything. Case in point—I know that she's done anal with Blake and loves it.

"Don't make me beat it out of you. It might not look like I could, but I absolutely could—and I will."

"Easy, killer. Don't strain yourself. I'll tell you what happened." And so I do. I spell it out for her, including most of the details that I know she'll want while keeping the really intimate things private out of respect for Garrett. When I'm finished, I'm shocked to see tears rolling down her cheeks. "What? *Why* are you crying?"

"I'm just so damned happy for you guys." She uses a napkin to mop up the flood. "This has been such a long time coming."

"Don't start planning the wedding quite yet." I hesitate before I share the thing that's been weighing on me since he left earlier. "I think he might want to keep it to just what's already happened."

"No way. You said it was amazing, right?"

"It was incredible—for both of us."

"He'll be back for more. Mark my words."

"I don't know... He was weird this morning. Noncommittal." That was the best word I could think of to describe the feeling he'd left me with at my house. "I asked if he wanted to work out together later, and he said maybe. Usually he says definitely or absolutely. Today he said maybe."

"And you're reading all kinds of things into that one word."

"It was more than that. I can't really explain it."

"What was the last thing he said?"

"He told me to have a good day."

"Before that."

I think about what we said. "We talked about the gym."

Honey rolls her hand with annoyance. "Before *that*."

"He told me to never let anyone make me think I'm anything less than perfect." Hours later, that sentence still makes my belly drop into free fall when I recall the way he looked at me when he said it, as if I am so very precious to him.

"Hmm," Honey says, looking away from me.

"Hmm what? What does that mean?"

"I'm not sure what it means."

"So you agree with me that a statement like that sounds more like the end than the beginning?"

"I wouldn't say that, for sure, but I agree it's not a slam-dunk this-is-the-start-of-something sort of statement."

I sag into my chair. I suspected as much, but hearing Honey confirm it has me... saggy.

"You're going to have to be patient and see how it plays out. But if I had to guess, a man who had the best sex of his life will be back for more."

"He never said it was the best sex of his life."

"Didn't he, Lo?" she asks softly. "He kept you there for thirty-six hours."

I want to latch on to that little kernel of hope, but life has taught me to be careful what I hope for. "After everything with my mother and Wayne, it's taken me such a long time to get back to feeling happy most of the time. I'm afraid to get my hopes up."

"I don't blame you for being cautious. I know how hard it is to be patient in situations like this. Remember how I almost lost my mind when Blake checked out after the accident? I didn't know if he was ever going to come around, but I was sure of only one thing."

The reminder of the awful accident they were in last year makes me feel sick. "What's that?"

"If he was ever going to come around, it had to be on his terms. I couldn't force it. He had to get there himself. The same is true for Garrett. There's no doubt that he cares for you. A *lot*. The question becomes whether you want the same things."

"I have no idea what he wants. He rarely ever talks about his hopes or dreams or the future or anything like that."

"It's possible he hasn't felt capable of having dreams for himself when he's been so busy seeing to his father's dream and making sure his family is cared for."

"That's a good point." She's definitely given me plenty to chew on.

"Tell me I have to go back to work now."

"Honey, get your fat ass out of my shop and go back to work."

"The fat-ass part was unnecessary roughness." She hauls said ass out of the chair with the grace of a water buffalo. "Flag on the play."

I giggle at her dramatic display as she lumbers to the back door. The alley behind my shop leads to the back door of hers. At the door, she stops and turns to me. "You know where I am if you need me, right? Any time. Pregnant or not. In labor or not."

Smiling, I say, "I know. Thank you."

"Love you."

"Love you, too." I blow her a kiss and see her out the door, watching her until she ducks into the door to the studio. Then I close the back door and slide the lock into place. Leaning against the door, I contemplate my next move. Garrett is nothing if not a creature of habit. He arrives at our gym five nights a week between six fifteen and six thirty. When he gets there tonight, I'll be waiting for him.

Satisfied to have a plan, I get back to work. I'm still catching up from yesterday, and I need to get out of here on time.

Garrett

I'm doing biceps curls when Blake comes into the gym. I nod at him across the wide-open room that's always busy this time of day. He ambles over to join me, choosing the fifty-pound weights and jumping into my workout already in progress.

"How you feeling?" he asks, eyeing me with suspicion that tells me he probably knows the truth about my "illness."

"Much better."

"Glad to hear it. I looked at your report on the spec houses, and you've got me convinced to dive in."

"You won't be sorry. With the school being built out there, you're sitting on a gold mine."

"I agree. I made an offer on the other fifteen parcels today, and the owner seemed excited. He was thinking he'd be selling them piecemeal, so fifteen at once was unexpected."

"He'll probably give you a deal for the quantity."

"That's what my broker said, too."

"Congratulations."

"Thanks, I think. Remind me why I thought this was such a good idea six months from now when I'm losing my mind at work and at home."

"You'll be fine. I have contacting recruiters for you on my to-do list for tomorrow."

"You might be able to scratch that off the list."

"Really? What happened?"

"It's the damnedest thing. You know my guy Mickey?"

"Uh-huh." As the keeper of the HR records for Blake's company, I have the lowdown on all his employees.

"His brother Jace is a construction supervisor for one of the biggest outfits in Dallas. At lunch the other day, Mickey mentioned his brother is looking to simplify a bit and starting to look around. I asked if he might be interested in working with us, and Mickey said he'd probably jump on it. He's talking to him this week to feel him out."

"That's great. If it works out, it'll save you the hassle of using a recruiter."

"If he comes down for a meeting, I'd want you there."

"Of course." Sitting on the tip of my tongue is the news about my interview in Austin, but I bite my tongue and keep the info to myself until I know for sure whether or not the job is going to happen. "I have to go to Austin Friday to Sunday. Do you mind being on call in case there's another plumbing disaster while I'm gone?"

"No problem," he says with a laugh. "Unless I'm in a delivery room, I'm all yours."

"Appreciate it."

"What's in Austin?"

Tell him. Tell him the truth. He'd understand. But would he? He relies so heavily on me to run his business that the news would probably freak him out, and he has enough on his mind with Honey about to pop and offering on the new development. I'll tell him afterward, if anything comes of it. "Taking a meeting for a client."

"Hope you'll have some fun while you're there."

"That's the plan."

"Hey, guess what I heard at the quick mart earlier when I was getting gas?"

"What's that?"

"Wayne Peterson's grandfather died. I wonder if he'll come home for the funeral."

Simon, one of the other gym rats we work out with regularly, pipes up. "He's back. I saw him at the bank earlier today."

It dawns on me that Lauren hasn't shown up to work out after indicating that she probably would. I drop the weights to the padded floor, and they land with a loud clank that startles Blake and the others working out nearby.

Suddenly, there's nothing more important to me in this world than getting to her before she hears this news from someone else. "I gotta go to her."

Nodding, Blake says, "Good call. You want me to come?"

"No, I've got it, but thanks."

"Call me later," he says as I bolt for the locker room, grab my clothes, wallet, phone and keys and run to the parking lot. As I throw the car into gear, I try to decide where to look first—home or the shop. After a second of debate, I head for the shop, because anyone can walk in through the front door there. At least at home, she'd have to choose to let him in—and she'd never do that.

CHAPTER 9

Garrett

It takes fifteen interminable minutes to make the short drive in what counts for "rush hour" in Marfa. While I wait for every light to cycle through twice, I try to call her four times while using the shirt I wore to work to mop up the sweat on my face. By the time I tear into the lot at Bloomsbury where Lauren's car is still parked, my anxiety is through the roof. It spikes even further when I realize the front door is still unlocked more than an hour after closing.

"Lauren!" The lights are on, but there's no sign of her in the storefront portion of the shop, so I round the counter and rush into the workroom. What I see there stops my heart. My beautiful Lauren, huddled in the corner, head down, arms wrapped around her knees, rocking back and forth. I'll fucking kill him with my bare hands, but first I have to see to her.

I drop to my knees in front of her. "Lauren. Sweetheart, it's me, Garrett." I tentatively place my hand over her freezing one, and she flinches. "Baby, it's me. You're okay. I'm here now. Hold on to me."

She moans like a wounded animal, and I have to remind myself to stay calm, to focus on her. The rage can wait.

I carefully wrap my arms around her, and she half leaps, half levitates into my embrace, nearly knocking me backward. But I manage to hold on to her as she breaks down into the kind of sobs that remind me all too much of the aftermath of her last go-round with Wayne.

"Shhh." I rub circles on her back and stroke her hair. "I'm here now. You're safe." I have no idea how long we sit there on the floor wrapped up in each other as she sobs, but after a while, she begins to calm ever so slightly, although she's still trembling violently. I'm not sure how to proceed. Do I ask what happened, or do I wait for her to tell me? I've got to know if he hurt her. In the softest voice I can manage, I say, "Are you hurt?"

She shakes her head.

Both our phones ring, but I ignore them. It's probably Blake calling me and Honey calling her. I'll update them as soon as I can. Right now, I'm all about Lauren.

"Sweetheart, will you look at me?"

Slowly, she raises her head to reveal her ravaged face. I grit my teeth to keep from roaring at the sight of her swollen eyes, bright red cheeks and... Are those fucking *bruises*?

I run my finger over the purple mark on her lower right cheek. There's a matching one on the other side. "Did he do this to you?"

"He... He came in to buy f-flowers for... for his grandfather's f-funeral." A sob shakes her. "I... I couldn't move. I was so scared. And then he... he grabbed my face and forced me to look at him."

I want to roar and rage. That he'd have the nerve to go anywhere near her is enough to make me want to see him dead.

"We're calling the police this time." She refused to cooperate in pressing charges the last time, saying she just wanted him gone, and if she pressed charges she'd have to deal with him for a long time—and he still could've gotten away with it after all that. "We can't let him do this."

"O-okay." The stammer, the sobs, the tears... They bring me back to the dreadful days that followed the first time he dared to lay his hands on her.

Tugging my cell phone from my pocket, I dial 9-1-1 and ask them to send police to Bloomsbury on Highland.

"What is your emergency?" the operator asks.

"My friend has been assaulted."

"Officers are on their way."

Lauren whimpers, and I wrap her up in my embrace again.

"Don't let go. Please don't let go."

The ache in my chest flares into a full-blown flame that threatens to incinerate me. "Never. I'll never let you go." As I hold her, the air conditioner comes on, triggering the delicate music of the wind chimes Lauren has displayed in the store. The joyful noise seems out of place in the midst of the drama unfolding around us.

In the distance, I hear approaching sirens. "Here they come, sweetheart. Do you feel able to talk to them?"

She shakes her head to say no.

"That's okay. I'll do the talking for you. Don't worry about anything. Just breathe."

The bells on the front door jingle as the cops come in. I'm relieved to hear my friend Brock Hernandez, chief of the Marfa Police Department, call for Lauren. "Back here, Brock."

He comes into the storeroom with a patrol officer and stops short at the sight of me sitting on the floor with Lauren in my arms. "What happened?" He's about six feet four inches of pure muscle, with dark hair and piercing blue eyes. Our friend Scarlett says the sight of his sexy face makes her want to drop her panties—information I could do without, but there you have it. From what I'm told by my female friends, Brock is hot, especially in uniform.

"Wayne Peterson happened—again. Came into the store and scared the hell out of her and then grabbed her face. He bruised and terrified her."

Brock's normally amiable expression goes hard as stone. To the officer with him, he says, "Put out the word for patrol to pick up Wayne Peterson at his mother's place." He rattles off the address from memory.

The patrolman goes outside to call it in.

Brock squats down next to us. "Hey, Lauren."

"Hi, Brock," she says, her voice muffled by my T-shirt.

"You want to tell me what happened?"

As promised, I speak for her. "She told me he came in to order flowers for his grandfather's funeral and caught her completely by surprise. She hasn't seen him since the night he attacked her. When she froze in shock, he took her by the face and squeezed hard enough to leave bruises. Tell me that counts as an assault."

"It definitely counts," Brock says. "Could I see, honey?"

Reluctantly, or so it seems to me, Lauren raises her face from my chest and shows her injured face to Brock.

He utters a low curse. "That son of a bitch never learns, does he?"

Lauren's eyes fill with tears, and she shakes her head.

"Do you need medical attention?" he asks.

"No. I'm okay."

"I'll be with her," I assure Brock.

"Tomorrow, I'll need you to come down to the station and file a formal report. Or I can come to you. Whatever works best."

"Could you come to her place in the morning?" I ask him, trying to make this as easy on her as possible.

"Of course." After a pause, he says, "You have to press charges this time, Lo. We can't let this happen again."

"I know," she replies in a soft, broken tone that makes the ache in my chest sharpen. I have so many emotions rushing through me right now that I can barely process them all. I want to protect her and hold her and love her and avenge her—all at the same time.

"I need to take some photos of the bruises, Lauren," Brock says. "Would that be okay?"

She glances at me, and when I nod in encouragement, she says, "Okay" in a small, defeated tone that breaks my heart.

Brock takes the photos quickly and with a minimum of fuss, which I appreciate.

"Will you see her home, Garrett?"

"Absolutely."

"One other question, Lauren. Do you have video surveillance in the store?"

She nods and points to the closed door off the storeroom. "It's in the office."

"Do I have your permission to review it?"

"Yes."

"We're going to be here awhile processing the scene. If you give me a key, I'll lock up when we're done."

"There's an extra set on my desk. They're the only keys on the desk."

"Great, thanks. You guys don't have to stick around if you want to go."

"Will you grab her purse from the office?" I ask Brock.

"You got it."

Because I want to get her out of here more than I want my next breath, I scoop her right up off the floor and settle her into my arms. She presses her face to my chest, as if the thought of anyone seeing her like this is more than she can bear.

I take the purse from Brock and make eye contact with him.

He nods to acknowledge the rage that I'm certain he can see all over my face and then holds the doors for me as I carry her to the parking lot.

Honey is waddling down the sidewalk between their storefronts as I load Lauren into my car. "Garrett! Oh my God! Blake called me. What happened?"

"Wayne Peterson paid her a visit."

Before my eyes, Honey goes pale and takes a stumbling step backward.

I grab her arm to keep her from losing her balance. "Are you okay?"

"Yes, sorry." She blinks back tears. "I just… I'm shocked."

"So is she. I'm taking her home."

"I'll wait for Blake, and we'll come over. We'll bring something to eat."

Because I know Lauren's other best friend needs to do something for her, I didn't object, even if I'd prefer to be alone with her. "Okay."

"Let me just…" She gestures to the passenger door of my car, and I step aside to give her access to Lauren.

Honey opens the door and bends—as much as she can, which isn't much—to speak to Lauren. I see Lo nod at whatever Honey says to her. Then Honey steps back, and again I take hold of her arm to help her find her bearings. If she doesn't give birth to this kid soon, I worry she's going to topple over at some point.

I'm about to offer to give her a ride back to the studio, but Blake's company pickup comes to a skidding stop at the curb, and he jumps out, running over to us. "Is she okay?" he asks of Lauren.

"She will be. He was rough with her and scared the hell out of her."

"Son of a bitch," Blake mutters.

"Brock is going to arrest him and charge him with assault."

"Thank fucking God. It's about time." He puts his arm around his wife and draws her into his embrace. "Come on, darlin'. Let's get you off your feet." As Blake leads Honey to the truck, I go around to the driver's side of my car and get in. "How you doing, sweetheart?"

"Okay."

"Blake and Honey are going to come over to check on you. I hope that's okay."

She nods. "It's fine. I'm sorry to make such a fuss."

"Don't you apologize for anything." My tone is harsher than I intended, and I immediately regret it. Placing my hand on top of her still-freezing hand, I soften my words. "None of this is your fault."

"I… When he came into the store, I-I couldn't believe what I was seeing. I thought I was hallucinating."

While keeping my hand over hers, I grip the steering wheel with my other hand so hard, it hurts. "I'm sorry you were so frightened, love."

"About one minute before he walked in the door, I got a call from the funeral home to let me know that Mr. Peterson had died, and they needed to order the funeral spray. That was all the warning I got that he might be back in town, and then he was in my shop."

I take comfort from the fact that she's talking about it and the stammer seems to be fading. Last time, it took two weeks for her to be able to talk about what happened, and the stammer had lasted a month. I have no doubt she's stronger now than she was then, but it still kills me that he hurt her again. I'd like to tear him apart with my own two hands, but I won't do that. I won't sacrifice myself to gain a moment's satisfaction. I'm always brought back to reality by the reminder of how many people rely on me. I don't have the luxury of being able to give in to my thirst for revenge. Rather, I'll focus on her and getting her through this.

An idea pops into my mind—the trip to Austin, the luxury suite, the spa, the pool, not to mention the wining and dining. The getaway could be just what she needs if we can make it happen. I'll mention it to her tomorrow when she's had time to process what happened today.

We pull into her driveway, and I run around to help her out of the car. "You want me to give you a lift?"

She gives me a small smile. "That's okay. I can walk."

I follow her up the stairs and wait for her to unlock the door before following her into the cool darkness of her home. Was it only this morning that we were here eating doughnuts and kissing the sugar off each other's lips? That seems like a lifetime ago now.

"Where do you want to be? Down here or upstairs in bed?"

"Here is fine." She curls up on the sofa, resting her head on a pillow with butterflies embroidered on it.

I cover her with the yellow throw that's slung over the back of the sofa and sit next to her, caressing her hair and taking notice of the darkening bruises on her cheeks. "How about some ice for your face?"

"That might feel good."

I kiss her forehead. "Coming right up." In the kitchen, I fill a plastic sandwich bag with ice and make sure it's completely sealed. I find a soft dishtowel in a drawer and bring that with me. I place the towel over the lower part of her face and then position the bag so it is split down the middle with ice applied to both sides. "How's that? Can you breathe?"

"Uh-huh. Feels good." She closes her eyes and takes a deep breath.

I brush the hair back from her face and let my fingertips venture over the upper curve of her left cheek. She is so very precious to me. How anyone could ever hurt or scare her is beyond me. Tears burn my eyes, and I close them to keep from breaking down. I haven't cried since my father died, and I can't start now or I might never stop.

Tuning in to my dismay, she curls her hand around my neck and gives a gentle tug, bringing my head down to rest against her shoulder. As she runs her fingers through my hair, I wonder how she ended up taking care of me rather than the other way around.

We stay that way until we hear Blake and Honey coming in the front door.

I raise my head to meet Lauren's gaze and kiss her forehead.

"Dinner's here," Honey calls out cheerfully.

By the smell of things, they've brought barbecue that makes my mouth water. I can't believe I'm actually hungry. "Do you feel like you could eat a little something, sweetheart?"

She removes the ice and towel from her face, which is red from the cold. "If they brought what I think they did, I could probably choke something down."

I say a silent thanks to Honey, who knew just what would appeal to Lauren. I help her up and hold her hand to walk her into the kitchen, where Blake and Honey have laid out dinner.

We hear the front door open again, and Lauren glances at me anxiously.

"Just me," Scarlett calls out. She comes into the kitchen and goes right to hug Lauren. "Where is he, and how can I stick an ice pick through his skull?"

Lauren laughs because how could she not? Scarlett is too much at the best of times, and absolutely perfect at the worst of times.

"Don't do that," Lauren tells her friend. "Don't any of you give in to the urge to get violent with him. Violence doesn't fix anything."

Leave it to Lauren to zero right in on what we're all thinking. I'm so proud of the way she's handling this latest encounter with Wayne. It's light years from how she was after the first time he hurt her, even if that incident was much more severe than this one. She's so much stronger now than she was then. Later, when we're alone, I'll tell her so.

We enjoy a lively dinner with our friends, who make an effort to act as if nothing is wrong. We're finishing up when Matt and Julie come in with their baby, Grace. Lauren reaches for the baby. Julie deposits her into Lauren's arms and then plants a kiss on Lauren's forehead.

Watching Lauren hug and kiss the squirmy baby has me rubbing that spot on my chest again. I should probably get that checked at some point. It's been pretty intense the last couple of days. It occurs to me that she's going to be a wonderful mother someday. Any child born to her will be one lucky kid. And where will I be when that happens? In Austin or some other far-flung glamorous location, growing my career and living the life I always dreamed of?

Surrounded by Lauren and my closest friends, watching our tribe band together in the midst of crisis, the thought of moving to Austin doesn't sound quite as good to me as it did only a few days ago. I'm so confused about everything, but I can't cancel the meeting that's been planned with such excitement by the company, and it would be good to get away with Lauren for a few days.

"So listen, guys," I say before I take another second to contemplate whether it's a good idea or not. It feels like a good idea, and that's enough for me. "I have to go to Austin tomorrow to meet with a potential new client. They're putting me up at the Four Seasons for the weekend, and I thought Lauren might come with me to take full advantage of the spa and pool while I'm working."

"Who's the client?" Blake asks, sounding suspicious.

"A restaurant group that's looking to expand. They saw the article about me in *Texas CEO* and hit me up." Part of that is true—the interest from the company I'm interviewing with came from the same article, which ran about a month ago and talked about the way I've grown my father's small-town business into a seven-figure operation in just six years. To Julie, I say, "Is there any way you could cover for Lauren at the shop so she can be away?" She's worked part time for Lauren over the years, filling in during the busy times.

"Absolutely. Grace and I would be happy to do that."

I glance at Lauren, who seems stunned by the turn of events. "What do you think, Lo? Are you up for a little getaway?"

"I... I don't feel right leaving Julie in charge on such short notice."

"Oh please," Julie says. "Give me something to do besides change diapers and breastfeed."

"She's stir-crazy," Matt adds gravely. "She'd love to get out of the house. You'd be doing us both a favor to let her work a few days for you."

Julie sends her husband a saucy smile that makes us laugh.

"Plus, Megan is there to help in the afternoons," Julie says. "I can handle it. Take a break, Lo. It'll do you good."

"I have to do Mrs. Smyth's grocery shopping on Sunday and count the money at church," Lauren says. "We have the special collection for the food bank."

"I'll take care of both those things," Honey says. "You're going to Austin."

To my horror, Lauren breaks down into sobs once again. I reach for her. "Sweetheart, what's wrong? Do you not want to go? We don't have to if you don't feel like it."

She shakes her head, and after taking a moment to get herself together, she says, "Y'all are the best friends any girl could ever have."

"We love you," Honey says bluntly. "There's nothing we wouldn't do for you. I'll help out at the shop, too. Go with Garrett. Have a good time. It'll do you good to get away for a few days."

"Can you do tomorrow and Saturday?" I ask Julie. The shop is closed on Sundays, so we only need coverage for two days.

"Yep. Consider it done."

"What about the five a.m. flower deliveries?" I ask Julie.

"I'll take care of it," Scarlett says. "I'm at the coffee shop by then anyway."

"Looks like you've got yourself a mini-vacation," I say to Lauren, whose bright smile lights up her teary eyes but then fades just as quickly.

"What?" I ask her.

"The bruises," she says softly, covering her face with her hands. "I can't go anywhere looking like this."

Her shame enrages me and tests my resolve to let Brock handle Wayne. I want to pummel him.

"I've got makeup that'll cover them," Scarlett says. "It's left over from my theater days. Don't worry. I'll fix you up and show you how to do it yourself. No one will know they're there."

"Oh. Okay."

"So we're going to Austin?" I ask her.

Nodding, she says, "I would love to go to Austin. Thank you for inviting me. I can't remember the last time I went anywhere."

When she agrees to come with me, the ache in my chest is replaced by a lighter feeling of flying higher than I ever have before. I don't really understand what it means, but I sure do like how it feels to know I have three days to spend with Lauren away from work and all my other responsibilities in Marfa.

I can't wait.

CHAPTER 10

Garrett

After everyone leaves, I finish cleaning up the kitchen and go looking for Lauren, bringing a fresh bag of ice with me. I find her upstairs in her room. She's changed into pajama pants and a tank top. Her hair is soft around her face, and her eyes have lost the haunted look they had earlier. I'm so relieved to see her recovering from the scare with Wayne relatively quickly.

"How're you feeling?"

"Surprisingly okay, thanks to you and the others. I'd be losing my mind if I had to deal with this alone."

"You'll never be alone." *But what about when you're in Austin, six and a half hours from her when something upsets or hurts her? What'll you do then?* I push that disturbing thought from my mind so I can focus on the present and what she needs right now. "How about some more ice?"

"Sure."

"Get comfy."

She gets into bed and sits back against a big pile of pillows.

Rounding the bed, I bring the ice pack and towel to her and help to position it. "Good?"

Gazing at me, she nods. She takes hold of my hand. "How did you know to come to the shop earlier?"

"I heard some guys talking at the gym about Wayne being back in town. I didn't think. I just ran."

"I'm so glad you did. I don't know what I would've done if you hadn't shown up when you did."

"I'm glad I was able to be there for you." After a pause, I ask her, "Do you want to be alone, or would you rather I stayed?"

She looks up at me with those big eyes that slay me. "Please don't go. I don't want to be alone."

I grasp her hand and give it a squeeze. "I'm not going anywhere, sweetheart."

"Thank you for that and for everything tonight."

"You don't have to thank me. I was hoping you'd want me to stay."

"I'm so excited about the trip to Austin. You hadn't mentioned that you were going."

"It came up earlier this week. I'm glad you can come. The client told me to bring a guest and make sure we take full advantage of the spa and the pool."

She sighs with pleasure, and the sound is so reminiscent of the hours we spent in my bed that my cock stirs for the first time all night. But tonight is not about that kind of pleasure. It's about comfort and safety and anything else she needs to get past what happened earlier.

"Do you mind if I grab a quick shower? I never took one after the gym."

"Of course not. Make yourself at home. Towels are in the closet."

"I'll be quick." In the bathroom, I'm not surprised to find bright yellow towels in the closet. I step into the shower I normally would've taken at the gym and turn my face up to the hot water, letting it rush over me while trying to summon the calm that Lauren needs from me. Tonight is all about her. After my shower, I put on only boxers and return to her bedroom to find that she has dozed off.

I carefully remove the ice pack and towel from her face and then stash them on the bedside table before turning off the light. I get into the other side of the bed and try to relax so I can sleep. But my mind is full of thoughts about the things

I'd like to do to Wayne Peterson, the interview in Austin and whether I should be concerned about the nagging ache in my chest.

At some point, I fall asleep and wake when Lauren curls up to me. I wrap my arm around her and hold her close to me, determined to protect her from ever being hurt again. But does that determination include turning down a huge career opportunity to stay close to her? That's one question I don't have the answer to.

*

Lauren's alarm goes off when it's still dark outside, startling me out of a disturbing dream in which I was chasing her, but she was continuously just out of my reach. I don't like the feeling that leaves me with as I rub my hands over my face.

She sits up and swings her legs over the side of the bed.

"Scarlett will get the flowers," I tell her.

"No need," she says, her voice noticeably stronger than it was last night. "I've got it."

I rest my hand on her shoulder. "Lauren… Take today and the weekend to get your head together before you go back to work."

She looks back at me, her eyes fierce with determination. "I absolutely refuse to let him make my precious shop that I've worked so hard to build from nothing into a place of fear. That is *not* going to happen. I'm going to get my damned flowers."

Well, all righty then. I drag myself out of bed to go with her.

"You don't have to get up yet."

"I'm coming with you."

"I don't need you to come with me. I've got this."

I love that her feistiness has returned overnight. I much prefer that to the condition I found her in at the shop last night. "What if *I* need to go with you?"

She shoots me an adorably withering look. "If you're going to put it that way…"

"I am putting it that way."

"Fine!" She throws up her hands. "Come with me."

"Gee, thanks for inviting me, babe."

She laughs, and I revel in the joyful sound. "I'm grabbing a quick shower to wake up, and then we can go."

"I'll be ready." While she's in the shower, I go out to my car to get the spare set of gym clothes from my bag so I can put on something clean. Her neighbor, Mrs. Smyth, is out retrieving her morning paper. She gives my bare chest a long look, licks her lips and smiles as she waves.

Um, okay... She's like seventy-something. I wave back and duck inside before she gets any big ideas about coming over to talk to me.

When I go back inside, Lauren is downstairs, her wet hair around her shoulders. She's wearing a short summer dress with battered cowboy boots, and my mouth goes dry at the sight of her sexy legs and those damned boots. God, they're hot.

"Did you really go outside without a shirt on? My neighbors will be all abuzz."

"Mrs. Smyth was licking her lips," I say with a scowl.

"The poor thing is only human. She's going to have to take an extra dose of her blood pressure medicine to recover from the sight of shirtless Garrett McKinley."

Lauren comes over to me and rests her hand flat over the exact spot on my chest that's been so damned achy lately. Just that quickly, I'm hard for her. What. The. *Fuck*? It usually takes much more than that with anyone else. What is it about her that makes me so damned crazy? I notice that she's put on the makeup that Scarlett went home to get for her last night, and the bruises are, in fact, invisible. Thank God for stage makeup.

"Shut up. She will not."

"She will, too," Lauren says in a low, sultry tone that does nothing to help the secondary ache in my groin. "You ought to be more responsible about your effect on womankind."

"I'll take that under advisement." I pull on a clean tank top. "Can we go get the damned flowers now?"

"By all means." She giggles as she goes by me out the door.

Smiling, I follow her downstairs. I'm so damned happy to see her in such a good mood today. It's a relief to know she hasn't fallen into the awful rabbit hole like she did the last time.

"Hey, Lo," I say to her when we're in my car on the way to the shop.

"Yeah?"

"I just want to say… I'm really proud of the way you're handling everything that happened yesterday."

"That means a lot coming from the person who saw the worst of it last time," she says, smiling sweetly at me.

"You're so much stronger now than you were then." And I'm so *fiercely* proud. The sentiment is so huge, it fills me to overflowing with emotions I can't seem to process. I find myself rubbing that damned ache in my chest. When we get back from Austin, I need to get that checked.

"Thanks for saying so. I didn't feel so strong last night when I fell apart at the shop."

"You didn't fall apart. You were understandably upset, but you've already bounced back."

"I'm not giving him any more of my time."

"Good. You shouldn't. And speaking of time, how much do you need at the shop today?"

"I've got arrangements for a rehearsal dinner and wedding to finish up, and I've got the orders for Mr. Peterson's funeral. I should be done by noon."

I glance over at her. "You're doing the funeral orders?"

"Why wouldn't I? Business is business, and Mr. Peterson was always nice to me. It's not his fault his grandson is a disgusting bully."

She's magnificent, and I love her. That realization comes over me like a wave crashing onto a beach. It knocks me over and sends me sideways. I *love* her—as much more than a friend. That was most definitely *not* the plan.

Is it a coincidence that the damned ache in my chest seems to let up at the same time this wave of understanding overtakes me?

"Garrett? Are you listening to me?"

I blink a couple of times to bring myself back to reality. Fuck. "What did you say?"

"I asked what sort of clothes I'll need for Austin."

"Oh, um, something to wear to a nice client dinner Saturday night. We can be more casual tonight. Otherwise, bikinis, lots of bikinis."

Out of the corner of my eye, I catch her eye roll. "Got it. One nice dress and a bunch of bikinis."

"That ought to do it. I'll try to finish up by noon, too, so we can get there in time for happy hour."

"I can't wait," she says, fairly bouncing in her seat with excitement.

I'm so thankful for the timing of the Austin trip. We both need a getaway.

We arrive at the shop and work together to bring in the buckets of flowers. I ask her the name of every one of them, and not only does she give me the commonly known name, but she supplies the Latin, too, which I find incredibly impressive. Her floral arrangements are works of art that are in hot demand around town. Bloomsbury designs feature the funky, colorful vibe that's so much a part of who Lauren is. While I wait for her to finish up, I take a long look around the shop, feeling like I'm seeing it for the very first time.

From the bright yellow walls that she sponge-painted herself with a technique she read about in a magazine, to the purple trim, to the colorful displays of silk butterflies, wind chimes, flowerpots, and other pottery, each item lovingly placed and arranged. She's poured her heart and soul into this business, and there's no way she'd ever want to leave it.

Her hand lands on my back, stirring me out of my thoughts. "Ready to go?" I ask her.

"In a minute. First, I could use your help with something in the workroom."

"Sure, whatever you need."

I follow her to the back room, where she turns to face me, looking up at me with those big, beautiful eyes. "I was wondering if you might be willing to help me create a new memory here, one that I'll enjoy thinking about…"

Bam. I'm hard. That's all it takes. "What did you have in mind?" I ask, even though I already know. I want to hear her say it.

She cozies up to me, walking me backward until my ass connects with the stainless-steel table that sits in the middle of her workroom. Then she cups my hard cock and squeezes, making me see stars. "Maybe something like this?"

"That works for me."

Smiling, she draws me down for a kiss that's all tongue and teeth and sizzling-hot desire. We skip the preliminaries and just dive in. It's an explosion of heat and need and pure, basic *want.* She practically crawls up the front of me in her enthusiasm for the kiss. I happily support her with my hands on her ass cheeks, which brings her heat into direct contact with my cock.

I groan into her mouth, and she bites down on my tongue, almost making me come. Breaking the kiss, I suck a deep breath into air-starved lungs and stare down at her. "You are so fucking beautiful." I turn us so her ass is on the table, and I come down over her as she lies back. "Do you have any idea how beautiful you are?"

To my disbelief, she shakes her head. "No one has ever told me that before."

"Those motherfuckers were fucking blind."

Her smile lights me up from the inside, filling me once again to the point of bursting. I can't stop staring at her, as if I'm seeing her for the first time, but in an all-new light now, the kind of light that burns so brightly, it lasts a lifetime.

She raises her hands to my face, her touch gentle and stirring. "Make love to me, Garrett. I need you so much."

Her request sparks something almost primal in me. My woman needs me. I move fast to pull down my shorts, and I don't bother to remove her panties. Why take the time when they can be pushed aside so easily? And then I'm inside her tight, wet heat, and her muscles are snug around my cock, and… *I'm so totally fucked.* I drop my head to her shoulder, close my eyes and focus on breathing. I can't leave her. That's as obvious to me in this moment as anything has ever been. Leaving her would be like leaving half of me behind—the best half of me.

I can't do it. I won't do it. If it's a choice between her and the big career I was always destined to have, fuck the career. Fuck Austin. Fuck it all.

Her fingers running through my hair send a current of electricity down my spine to my balls, which tingle with growing urgency. "Garrett? Are you okay?"

"Yeah, baby. It's all good." And it will be. I'll see to that. But first things first. I raise myself up and cup those gorgeous ass cheeks, my fingers digging into dense flesh as I thrust into her, going deep and then retreating, teasing her with twists of my hips that make her scream from the pleasure. I pound into her so hard that the table moves closer to the far wall.

I can tell she's on the verge of coming, and I could easily help her along, but I decide I'd rather draw it out a while longer to make sure this memory is permanently seared in her mind. I pull out of her abruptly, making her gape with surprise. I pick her up and turn her around so she's standing on the floor, facing the table. With my hand on her back, I bend her at the waist and enter her from behind. Fuck, *yes.* I can go so much deeper this way.

I start the build all over again, driving into her over and over again, our flesh slapping together and her supple cheeks jiggling with every thrust. She's so fucking hot and wet and tight. God, *so* tight. Her pussy muscles flutter around my cock like a hand job, only so much better.

I reach down to where we're joined to lube up my middle finger, which I then drive into her ass. She comes immediately, so hard she nearly breaks my freaking finger. She screams bloody hell, and I love it. I love every fucking second of it, especially the part where I come so hard my vision goes black for a second. I bite my tongue to keep from blurting out every thought in my head, all of them involving the two of us doing this for the rest of our lives.

When my head stops spinning, I withdraw from her and help her up. "How was that for a better memory of the workroom?"

She pushes her hair back from her face, which is flushed and sexy as she smiles up at me. "That'll do."

I smile back, like a dopey lovesick fool. What the fuck took me so long to figure out that the only thing I need to be happy is *her*? I don't need a big job or a big city or anything other than *her*. I should cancel the trip to Austin. I should call the CEO's assistant… What was her name again? I should call her and tell her I can't make it after all because, it seems, I already have the life I was intended to live, right here in Marfa with Lauren.

But I promised her the weekend away, and the people there have made plans. I suppose at the very least I owe them the courtesy of hearing them out. So that's what I'll do. I'll hear them out, and then we'll come home where we belong. The decision is a relief after days of feeling like I'm all over the place—here, there and nowhere, up in the air in a weird state of limbo. My path forward is now crystal clear and staring up at me with a quizzical look.

"Are you okay?"

"I'm good." I kiss her. "No, I'm great, in fact." She's still staring at me when I go to the sink to wash my hands. I feel like I could climb mountains or take on the world or do anything as long as I have her to come home to at the end of the day. And at the end of this day, we're going to Austin for a whole weekend together. I can't wait.

*

We leave Marfa later than expected due to Lauren having to give a statement to Brock as well as a "crisis" with Sierra, who decided to stay out all night—without telling my mother. Mom is freaked out about her having sex with her boyfriend and getting pregnant, but do you think Mom is willing to talk to her about that? Nope. That special joy fell to me, and it was every bit as awkward as you might imagine. I cringe just thinking about it.

"You're quiet over there," Lauren says as we head east on I-10.

If we don't encounter traffic, we should be there by eight, in time to enjoy a nice dinner, perhaps in our suite rather than going out. "I'm still trying to scrub my brain of the memories of talking to Sierra about sex."

She responds with a low chuckle and a hand on my leg, both of which remind me of the fact that we have almost four hours to go before I can hold her and kiss her and make love to her again. "Poor baby," she coos. "It's not easy being you, is it?"

"No, it isn't. Thank you for noticing."

"What did Sierra have to say?"

"She assured me she hasn't had sex with anyone and doesn't plan to, not that it's any of my business. And she reminded me once again that I'm not her father and to quit acting like I am."

"I bet she doesn't mind you acting like her father when she needs money."

"You would win that bet."

"You're never going to want kids of your own after helping to raise her and Lola," she says with a sigh.

I find it interesting that she frames that comment as a statement and not a question. "I don't know. They don't come out as teenagers, do they?"

"Often they arrive as infants, actually."

"Is that right? In that case, I might be convinced to give it a whirl. I actually liked Sierra and Lola when they were babies. Remember when my mom told us we had to stop referring to them as 'the babies' when they were in middle school?"

"I do!" She laughs. "That used to make them so mad."

"They'll always be the babies to me. The thought of Sierra having sex makes me want to kill the randy little motherfucker she's dating."

"I hate to break it to you, but she's going to do it eventually."

"Not if I can get her into a convent first."

"Ha! Let me know how that goes."

In more than six hours, we never run out of things to talk about. We laugh about the funny things that have happened in the past as well as the staggering array of reasons my family has called on me over the years, such as the time Sierra decided to jam a peanut butter and jelly sandwich down the toilet. Lauren points out the ongoing toilet theme, which has us both cracking up.

It's so easy with her. We know all the same people. We've been close friends since sixth grade. We've been through everything together. At some point, without me quite realizing it, she became the other half of me. Now that I've figured out what was right in front of me all along, I feel calmer and more at peace than I have in a long time.

After we get through this weekend, I'm going to talk to her about making some plans.

We're an hour outside of Austin when we receive a call from Brock. I take it on the Bluetooth and let him know he's got both of us.

"I'm glad I caught you guys," he says. "I wanted to let you know that we've charged Wayne with simple assault for what happened yesterday at the shop."

"There was nothing simple about that assault," I reply testily.

"I know," Brock says with a sigh. "But it was the best I could do under the circumstances."

"Because I didn't press charges last time, right?" Lauren asks.

I hate that her voice sounds small and timid, the way it gets any time she talks about Wayne.

"It's not your fault, Lauren," Brock assures her.

"Sure it is," she says. "If I hadn't let him off the hook then, we could've nailed him now."

I place my hand on top of hers, which is still on my leg. "Will he do any time?" I ask Brock.

"No. Simple assault is a misdemeanor, but I let him know that Lauren will be filing for a restraining order that'll require him to stay at least a thousand feet from her. He won't be stopping in to buy any more flowers. I'll see to that."

"Thank you, Brock," she says. "I want you and Garrett to know that if I had it to do over again, I would've charged him last time."

"You did what was best for you at the time," Brock says. "No one can fault you for that. I'm allowing him to attend the funeral, and then I'll personally make sure he leaves town and stays gone this time. He's been told he's not welcome back here for any reason."

Lauren nods with approval. "Thanks again, Brock. I really do appreciate your help and support."

"Just doing my job."

"And being a good friend, too," she says.

"That's my pleasure. You guys have a nice time in Austin. Try to relax."

"We will," I say. "Talk to you when we get back."

"I'll be here."

I disconnect the call and glance over at Lauren, who's staring out the window as she gnaws on her bottom lip. "You okay?"

"Surprisingly, yes. I'm actually relieved."

"Because he's being charged?"

"That and I don't have to worry about him coming back anymore."

"You've been stressing out about that?"

"Every day since the last time I saw him. I knew he'd resurface eventually."

"Why didn't you say anything?"

"I didn't want everyone to worry or hover. You've all got your own businesses to run. And don't try to deny that you would've hovered."

I would've hovered. She's right about that. "Okay. I won't deny it."

"You know what the very best part of my whole life has been?"

"What's that?" I ask, desperately wanting to know.

"You and Honey and Blake and Scarlett and Matt and Julie and Brock and the rest of our friends in Marfa. You guys are my family, and I love you all so much."

That larger-than-life feeling from before blooms once again inside me, the feeling I now recognize as love, and not the kind of love between friends. No, this is much bigger than that, and soon, when the time is right, I'll tell her so. "We love you, too," I say simply, even though nothing about my feelings for her is simple. Not anymore. If I'm being honest with myself—and I always try to be—it hasn't been simple between us in a long time, probably since the aftermath of her breakup with Wayne, when she wanted me and only me, and there was nowhere else on earth I would've rather been than with her when she needed me.

I try not to think about when or how she turned to Blake after the intensity of the Wayne situation waned and we resumed our lives. She said it didn't mean anything with him, and I have to believe her. I can't let myself think about her being with any other guy, even my good friend. But there again was another opportunity with her that I missed out on. She might not have turned to Blake if I'd stepped up to be more to her than a good friend after her marriage imploded. I won't make that same mistake again.

I like being needed by her. It's an entirely different proposition than being needed by my mother, my sisters, my employees or clients, and I hope she needs me for the rest of our lives.

CHAPTER 11

Garrett

"What do you feel like doing first when we get to Austin?" I ask her after a comfortable period of silence.

"I really need to hit the gym, even if it's just for half an hour. I haven't worked out in days."

"You never have to talk me into that." It's another of many things we have in common—our obsessive commitment to fitness.

After we arrive at the Four Seasons in Austin and check into our enormous, elegant suite, we change and head directly to the fitness center, where we spend an hour sweating off any remaining stress we brought with us. We've worked out together so often that we exchange few words as we spot each other through the weightlifting portion of the program, going through the paces like the well-oiled team we are.

Again, I'm struck by the fact that it took me so long to accept that she is my destiny. All this time, we've been dancing around the truth while slowly but surely becoming essential to each other. I like to think of myself as a pretty sharp guy, but this situation is proof that I can be as obtuse as the next guy when it comes to women. Or I suppose I should say when it comes to the woman who matters most. The rest of them weren't all that mysterious to me. I knew what they wanted, and I gave it to them.

Everything is different with Lauren, and the funny part is that it always has been different with her.

"Remember the time Bruce the Dick Dickenson tipped your lunch tray over in middle school?" I ask her when we're in the elevator on the way back to our top-floor suite.

"How could I forget? You got suspended for beating him up in the cafeteria."

"I'd do it again in a New York minute. He made you cry."

"Because I didn't have the money to buy a second lunch, and I was starving." She looks up at me. "What made you remember that?"

"I was thinking about how far back we go, and how we've always been special friends."

"Yes, we have. You were the first person in my whole life who ever defended me. Did you know that?"

I'm struck dumb by her heartfelt words. "No," I say gruffly. "I didn't know."

"I spent most of my childhood cleaning up my mother's messes. She was never there for me. I saw my dad once a year, if that. He was never there for me. The day you beat up Bruce the Dick was the first time anyone ever stuck up for me. I've never forgotten it."

"You know what I remember most about that?"

"What?"

"That I wanted to *kill* him for making you cry. I was twelve, and I think if the teachers hadn't pulled me off him, I might've actually killed him. I've only ever felt that way two other times, when Wayne put you in the hospital, and again last night."

She wraps her hands around my arms and leans her head on my shoulder until the elevator lands on our floor.

I open the door to our room and let her go in ahead of me. When the door clicks shut behind us, I say, "Hey, Lo?"

She turns to me. "Hmm?"

"I wish I'd never given Wayne the chance to hurt you, that I'd done something... about this, about us... a long time ago."

"We weren't ready for this then. We would've messed it up."

I shake my head. "No, we wouldn't have."

She takes a few steps to close the distance between us, sliding her arms around my waist.

I rest my hands on her shoulders and gaze down at her, feeling like I'm truly *seeing* her for the first time, even after all these years.

"You have always been my hero, Garrett. Even when I was married to Wayne, you were the one I leaned on because I knew you loved me no matter what."

"I did love you," I whisper. "I *do* love you. I love you so much. You'll never know how much."

"I've always known, and I love you just as much. I have for as long as I can remember." Then she kisses me, and I lose myself in her, surrendering to the pull to her that is too powerful to resist. I'm done fighting it. I don't want to fight. I just want to make her happy and keep her safe every day for the rest of our lives. As she wraps herself around me and nearly brings me to my knees with desire, everything else fades away and there's only her.

Without breaking the kiss, I lift her and carry her to the nearest flat surface, which happens to be the dining room table in the fancy suite. I lay her out on the table and bend over her, my cock snug against the heat of her core. For the first time in the six years since my father died, I feel like I'm exactly where I'm supposed to be with the person I'm supposed to be with, and I finally have the answers to the most important questions.

Lauren.

She's the answer to every question.

I break the kiss and gaze down at her, noticing that she seems as stunned by the desire pulsing between us as I am.

"I probably stink," she says with a wry smile.

I shake my head. She always smells good, even when she's sweaty. "I definitely stink."

"No, you don't." She squirms restlessly under me, letting me know what she wants as badly as I do. With one arm propped on the table, I remove her shorts and then my own.

"*Garrett*," she says, her urgency fueling mine.

I grasp those ass cheeks that are the stuff of fantasy and angle her to accept my cock. I pause for a fraction of a second, only long enough to make her moan, and then I slam into her, going all the way to the hilt in one thrust.

She comes immediately, her fingernails sinking into my back and her internal muscles massaging me intimately.

I wait her out, and then I start to move. I've never fucked her as hard as I do now that I've given myself permission to love her, to want her, to need her. I need her so fucking bad. The words pour out of me in a flood of thoughts and emotions that can no longer be contained. I, who rarely talks during sex, let go with every thought inside my head. "I love you so fucking much. Every beat of my heart is for you—only you—and it always has been. No one will ever love you the way I do."

I'm completely out of control, and the funny thing is, I know it and don't care. I don't care that I'm laying myself bare before her, surrendering to the fifteen-year slow burn that erupts like fireworks in the night sky. "I want to marry you and have babies with you and watch them turn into obnoxious teenagers with you. I want every day and every night and every morning with you. I want to sleep with you and make love to you and fuck you and devour you and protect you from ever being hurt again and have every fucking thing with you."

A broken sob erupts from her, stopping me in my tracks. "Baby, don't cry. Please don't cry."

"You have n-no idea how long I've waited to hear you say th-those things to me. Of course I'm going to cry."

I gather her into my arms, lift her off the table and drop into one of the chairs that surround the table. She settles on top of me, my cock still deep inside her as she gazes down at me.

"I love you, too. I love you as so much more than my very best friend, and I think I have since you beat up Bruce the Dick for me."

I tighten my hold on her and bury my face in the elegant curve of her neck. "We've wasted so much time."

"No," she says, "we were busy getting to a place where we were ready for this."

Cupping her ass cheeks, I lift her slightly and then let her drop back onto my cock. I do it again, raising her a little higher this time before letting her fall. Each time, she expels a breath when she lands, and her muscles flutter around my cock.

Tears continue to slide down her cheeks, and I brush them away with my lips.

She gazes into my eyes as I look up at her in a moment of utter clarity. All this time I've been running toward something, but it wasn't what I thought it would be. I don't need a big fancy corporate career in a city far from home to feel whole. No, all I need is this tiny woman with the big personality, a heart of gold and a love that will last forever.

I grab the back of the tank top she wore to the gym and work it up and over her head to gain access to her breasts. Holding one in my hand, I take her nipple into my mouth and suck hard, running my tongue back and forth across the tight tip. The combination has her riding me frantically, chasing her orgasm. I keep it up until her inner muscles clamp down on me and take us both flying off the cliff, and this time, the sense of falling is the greatest feeling I've ever had.

I'm falling for her. I have fallen for her, completely and totally, and the fall doesn't seem so scary when I take it with her.

She clings to me in the aftermath, her chest tight against mine, her face wet with new tears that dampen my face, too. Or maybe those are my tears. Who knows, and what does it matter?

"Did you mean it?" she asks in a small voice after a period of silence.

"Every word."

"Garrett," she says on a long exhale. "You really want to marry me?"

"That's the very least of what I want with you, if you'll have me."

"If I'll have you," she says with a laugh as she pivots her hips. "I believe I already have you. Right where I want you."

My heart expands almost painfully in my chest, testing the boundaries of this newfound ability to love so greatly. Until now, I had no idea I was even capable of such powerful emotions. Growling playfully, I nip her neck and squeeze her ass cheeks. Have I mentioned that I'm obsessed with her ass? "You've gotten me very dirty. How about a shower?"

"Yes, please."

I pick her up and carry her to the bathroom.

"Oh my God," she says of the giant claw-footed soaking tub that occupies half the bathroom. "That tub! Can we?"

"Of course we can."

I continue to hold her until the water is warm and then step into the tub with my precious cargo still in my arms. She adds some bubble bath from the basket of luxurious products provided by the hotel and then relaxes into my embrace.

"Is this a dream?" she asks.

"No, baby. It's not a dream. It's a dream come true." I think about the daylong meeting planned for tomorrow and wonder how or when I'll tell them it's all for naught. I feel badly for wasting their time, but I would've felt worse about canceling at the last minute after they went to so much trouble to arrange everything.

I want to tell Lauren why I really came to Austin, but again, what does it matter when I'm not going to take the job? She doesn't need to know that I ever considered leaving Marfa for something bigger or supposedly better than what I have there. I wouldn't want her to think that she kept me from chasing my dreams. My dreams have changed. It's that simple.

I wash and condition her hair, and then she does the same for me with scrupulous attention to detail.

"What kind of a wedding do you want?" I ask her.

The question causes her to freeze, her gaze shifting to meet mine, as if to check whether I'm for real. I'm so for real. I've never been more for real in my life. "I... um, I don't care. Whatever you want."

"No way. Don't do that. You know exactly what you want and you probably have for years. Spill it."

"If I could have anything I wanted—"

"You can."

"I'd want to do it at the Paisano," she says, referring to the local hotel that is a national historic landmark. "I've delivered flowers to countless weddings there, and every time, I picture my own wedding there someday, which is silly since I've already been married."

"Tying the knot with Wayne fucking Peterson at the courthouse doesn't count as a wedding."

"No, but unfortunately, the marriage was legal. Biggest mistake I ever made. You know that, right? I never should've married him or even dated him. But you were away at college, and I couldn't live with my mom anymore. I just couldn't. He seemed like a better alternative."

"I get it, babe. I've always understood the why of it, even if it broke my heart to hear you'd married him."

"I never intended for that to happen. I didn't know you thought of me that way. If I had, everything would've been different."

"We both have our regrets, Lo. I should've said something. Do you know how many times I've thought about Christmas break my senior year of college when you told me he'd asked you out and I didn't say anything? I should've told you then not to go out with him, but my life was still a gigantic question mark at that time. I had no idea where I was going to end up or if I was going to get a good job or anything. I didn't think it would be fair to tell you to wait until I worked out my shit."

"I would've waited," she says, tipping her head back so she can see me. "If you'd given me the slightest encouragement, I would've waited for you."

"I'm sorry that I didn't. My only excuse is that I was young and dumb and thought I had all the time in the world to work things out with you. There was never a time, even when I dated other people, that you weren't right there, in the back of my mind like the pot of gold at the end of the rainbow or something like that."

"Awww, that's so sweet."

I scowl at her. "I am not *sweet*."

"You are if I say you are. And not only are you sweet, you're poetic, too. I'm the pot of gold at the end of your rainbow."

I make dramatic gagging noises that crack her up. "Shoot me now."

"No, thank you. I'd much rather kiss you."

"I'd be fine with that."

She turns over to face me, and I hold her close for a soft, sweet kiss that has my heart racing and my cock throbbing once again. How does she do that so easily? I sweep the wet hair back from her face. "Did you ever picture the groom at your Paisano wedding or just the dress and flowers?"

"I never dared to picture the one man I would've chosen if I could have anyone I wanted."

"Why not?"

"I was afraid to go there, like I might jinx it or something."

"Do I know this guy?"

She laughs—hard—and I fall even further than I already have. I keep thinking I've reached the full potential of how far I can possibly fall only to discover there's more. So much more.

Her fingers sift through my hair, straightening it. "He has the most gorgeous dark hair and eyes so brown they almost look black until the sun hits them just so, and then you can see the speckles of gold. His skin is always tanned, even in the middle of what passes for winter in West Texas. He has muscles on top of his muscles. He'd do anything for anyone and has proven that time and again with the way he takes care of his family and friends, always putting the needs of others ahead of his own. He's *so* smart that his clients can't imagine having to run their businesses without his help. And on top of all that, he's the sexiest, sweetest, best man I've ever known, and I've been in love with him since the sixth grade when he beat up the bully who made me cry."

Nothing in my life has ever humbled me more than she just did. "He's a very lucky man to have had someone like you love him for so long."

She shakes her head. "I'm the lucky one."

"We're both lucky." I kiss her again and notice how much different it feels to kiss her now that I know she loves me and she knows I love her. It's bigger, somehow, greater... "So a wedding at the Paisano as soon as possible?"

She nods. "That would be perfect."

"I'll get you a ring, and we'll make it official. Soon."

"You don't have to. Let's spend the money on the wedding."

"You can have both, and I want you to have a ring."

"Where will we live? Your place or mine?"

"Either is fine with me, or we can sell them both and get something together. Whatever you want."

"Are you always going to be this agreeable?"

"Are you always going to be my wife?"

"That's the goal."

"Then yes, as long as you're my wife, I'll be your agreeable husband."

"My husband," she says on a long sigh as she lays her head on my shoulder. "I can't believe this is happening."

"Believe it, baby. We're going to have it all, everything you've ever wanted and things you haven't even dreamed of yet." I would do everything within my power to make sure of that.

"What about babies?" she asks in the small voice that's far too reminiscent of the months that followed Wayne's attack.

"As many as you want. And I don't want you to ever be afraid to ask me for anything. You own me. You always have. I'm only sorry it took me so long to figure that out."

"This was the way it was meant to be. I believe that."

"I need to get you out of this tub before you turn into a prune on me."

"We can't have that."

She gets up first, and I follow her into the shower to rinse off the bubbles. Then I wrap her in a big white fluffy towel and thoroughly dry her.

"I'm going to dry my hair real quick, or it'll be huge."

"I like your hair huge."

"Said only a man from Texas."

"You know it, darlin'," I say in an exaggerated drawl. "We like our women easy, with big breasts and bigger hair."

She snaps the towel at me and just misses my junk. "Pig."

Laughing, I jump out of the way and cover the family jewels with my own towel. "If you want babies, sweetheart, you'd better be nice to my boys." We stand together at the vanity, me shaving while she dries her hair—naked. I can't take my eyes off her beautiful tits, which jiggle with every move she makes, and it takes a lot of movement to dry her long hair.

"You're going to cut yourself again if you keep staring at me rather than the mirror."

"I'd so much rather stare at your luscious tits than my ugly mug."

"I'm quite fond of your ugly mug, and I don't want any more blood. Pay attention to what you're doing with that razor."

It's all so... domestic. Even though we're far from home, she may as well already be my wife for the way she keeps me centered and grounded. That's a role she's played for years without me even realizing it. I feel sort of stupid that it took me so long to open my eyes to what was right in front of me.

My dad used to say we can't change the past. All we have is right now. Make the most of it. That's what I intend to do. "You want to go out to eat or order room service?"

"Would you care if we stayed in?"

"I'd actually prefer it. We're going out tomorrow night anyway."

"Where're we going?"

"The Austin Country Club."

"Who are these clients?"

"It's a high-tech firm looking for a point of contact in Marfa and the surrounding area." I realize after I say it that I've told her a different story than I told Blake. I'm digging a hole for myself that could get me in trouble if I'm not careful.

"Ah, I see. Nice of them to put us up in such high style for the weekend."

"Uh-huh." This would be a good time to tell her why we're really here, but I still don't want her to know that I was so intent on leaving Marfa that I went so far as to hire a headhunter. I think that would hurt her, and I can't do that to her. I'm going to turn down their offer and thank them for a nice weekend. No harm, no foul. That's the plan.

We enjoy a delicious dinner delivered to our room and watch a movie in bed that doesn't hold my interest. How could it when Lauren is soft and fragrant and naked in a bed with me? I run my hand up and down her arm, smiling at the outbreak of goose bumps that have her quivering.

"Quit tickling me," she says, her breath warm against my chest.

"I'm not tickling you. I'm touching you."

"Same thing." Her dramatic yawn is a reminder that she's tired, and I should leave her alone, but now that everything is settled between us, I want her even more than I did before. I lightly drag my fingertips over her arm, knowing that will definitely tickle her. "*Garrett!*"

"Hmm?"

"Stop!"

"Make me."

She surprises the hell out of me when she pounces, grabbing my hands and pinning them over my head while crushing her breasts to my chest.

"Is that supposed to discourage me?" I ask, raising my hips to show her what her demonstration has caused.

"Does he ever take a break?"

"Not when you're naked and anywhere near him."

"I suppose you don't get a reputation for being a sex god without having a *lot* of sex."

"You know it, baby, so you'd better protect my reputation by seeing to him whenever he's feeling needy."

She rolls her eyes. "Is that what kind of wife you think I'm going to be?"

"Hell yes. You have me at your mercy. At the very least, you should be... merciful."

"Is that right?"

"Uh-huh." God, this is fun. I feel like I've hit the jackpot because I get to have a sleepover with my very best friend every night for the rest of my life. I pull at the tight hold she has on my arms, encouraging her to release me, but she doubles down and slides her damp heat over my hard cock. "Lauren..."

"Yes?"

"Come on..."

"Is someone feeling eager?"

"Explosive is more like it."

"So it's okay for you to tease me, but it's not okay when I do it?"

"Exactly."

She laughs, and the light that infuses her pretty eyes stops my heart. I love when she's happy and laughing and teasing me. "Is this what you want?" She lowers herself onto my cock, surrounding my sensitive flesh with her tight wet heat.

"Yeah," I gasp, desperately trying to hang on to my control as she shreds me with every move of her hips, every drag of her nipples over my chest. The sensations come at me fast and furious. This is going to be over before it begins unless I can take control. I break free of her hold and wrap my arms around her, turning us so I'm on top of her.

"Hey! No fair. You can't just overpower me like that."

"I won't make a habit of it," I say through gritted teeth. "I promise." I hook my arms under her legs, opening her to my fierce possession. I pinch her left nipple between my fingers and place the thumb of my other hand on her clit, pressing it in time with my deep thrusts.

The position renders her helpless to do anything other than take what I'm doling out. Her body is angled upward, which allows me to go even deeper. I remain deeply embedded in her as I pinch her nipple and manipulate her clit. The combination has her gasping and trembling madly. I don't let up, playing her body like a maestro until she screams from the orgasm that rips through her.

Her pussy clamps down on my cock so hard, I see stars, but I don't let myself go. Rather, I power through the storm of her release without giving in to my own. She returns to me in stages. First, a deep breath, then a sigh and finally a flutter of lashes as she opens her eyes to look up at me with wonder and satisfaction.

"Wow," she says on a whispery exhale.

"Wow is right. How about another one?"

"I don't think I can."

"Is that a challenge?"

She groans and wraps her arms around me, encouraging me with her legs around my hips and her fingers in my hair. "I know better than to challenge you."

I laugh and nearly lose my groove for a second before recovering my mojo. I'm determined to coax another orgasm from her before I let her sleep. This time, I use my words to cajole her. "I can't believe you thought for one second you weren't good at this. You're so tight and hot and wet. Your pussy grabs my cock like a glove and squeezes. I have to fight to not come every second I'm inside you." I grasp her ass and pound into her. "I could fuck you all night and never get enough of how it feels to be inside you. I want to spend entire days doing nothing but this."

A flush of heat travels from her breasts to her face. Her lips part, and her breath catches. Sensing she's close, I prop myself up on one arm and use my free hand to reach between us to coax her. It takes only one brush of my finger over her clit to send her flying.

My name escapes her lips like a broken-sounding oath.

I close my eyes, bury my face in the fragrant silk of her hair and let go. The force of my release leaves me shaking like a newborn in the aftermath.

Lauren's hands on my back soothe and comfort me as I try to recover my bearings.

Christ have mercy.

"Your reputation is very well earned."

Her comment makes me laugh even as I try to suck greedy breaths into my air-starved lungs. "I was in training for you."

"That training is over now. You got me?"

"I will never again touch anyone but you."

"Promise?"

I raise my head to meet her gaze and nod. "Easiest promise I'll ever make. If I have you, I have everything I need."

She looks up at me with her heart in her eyes. "Same goes."

I'm at once relieved and euphoric and hopeful, more hopeful than I've been in the six long years since my life took a sudden and unexpected detour. In her arms, I'm finally back on track and right where I belong.

CHAPTER 12

Garrett

At nine the next morning, I leave Lauren sleeping in the suite with a wake-up call set for nine thirty so she can eat the breakfast I ordered her before her spa appointments begin at ten thirty. In the lobby, I meet the driver who was sent to retrieve me and deliver me to the Austin headquarters of Social-NET. The company has revolutionized social media management with its all-in-one app that allows the user to be present on all platforms simultaneously.

I've read every word that's been written about the company, its proprietary technology and the staggering projections for the initial public offering expected early next year. At any other time in my life, I'd want to be part of the exciting future of this company. But all at once, my future is looking plenty exciting without a major career move thrown into the mix.

The hard sell begins with the driver, who points out a variety of landmarks and selling points on the way to the glass office tower in Downtown Austin. Marilyn, Mr. Dutton's pretty, dark-haired assistant, who is younger than I thought she'd be, greets me in the lobby with a firm handshake and an enthusiastic welcome.

"We're so happy to have you with us today," she says as we walk toward a bank of elevators where she uses her badge to gain access to the top floors.

"Thanks for having me. Before we go too much further, I wondered if I could possibly have a private word with Mr. Dutton."

"We're actually on a pretty tight schedule this morning. I'd be happy to see if I could get you some time alone with him after lunch."

I sag ever so slightly against the back of the elevator, resigned to going through the motions before I get the chance to tell them that this isn't going to happen.

The day unfolds like a natural disaster, or at least that's how it seems to me. They are determined to blow me away, and they nearly succeed. I'm dazzled by the people I meet, the presentations, the sales pitch, the facilities and the R&D that's being done to further expand upon the technology. It's overwhelming and interesting and so bloody tempting that I nearly forget my resolve to say thanks but no thanks.

A catered lunch is provided to the entire team, who include me in their conversations as if I'm an old friend who's been invited to spend the day with them rather than a potential employee. I like every one of them. They're my kind of people—smart, ambitious, funny, clever and young. The day is like a surreal rendition of *It's a Wonderful Life*, a look at what my life might've been like had my father not dropped dead.

And then it's down to Gerald Dutton and me, alone in his massive corner office with its panoramic view of the Colorado River. He's in his fifties with silver hair and vivid blue eyes that crackle with intelligence and humor and unexpected warmth. I like him as much as I like everyone else I've met today.

"Well," he says, handing me a glass of bourbon as he joins me in the sitting area of his massive office. "What do you think of my team?"

"The word 'impressive' doesn't do them justice."

Judging by the big smile that lights up his affable face, he is pleased by my assessment. "Couldn't agree more."

"Mr. Dutton..."

"Call me Jerry. Please."

"Thank you. Jerry... This has been a truly incredible day. My mind is well and truly blown."

"Then we've done our jobs," he says. "Before you go any further, take a look at this." He hands me a folder that contains an offer letter. A base salary of one million per year with stock options tied to the IPO that alone would make me a very rich man. I'm speechless. I can only stare at the single sheet of paper that offers everything I'd been looking for in a potential executive-level position—and much more than I'd dared to hope for.

"Why me?" I ask him. Even if it's not going to happen, I still want to know what drew him to me.

"Long before the recruiter reached out to us, I'd read about the success you've made of your father's company. Like you, I lost my father at a critical juncture in my life, and I know what it's like to feel set adrift by the loss of my anchor. Everything I've done since then has been with the goal of making him proud in the back of my mind. I'm sure you can relate to that."

"I can," I say gruffly, taken aback by his insight as much as his thoroughness.

"I need someone like you on my team, Garrett. The last two CFOs we hired haven't had the vision or the drive I need in that position. You've turned a small-town practice into a thriving business in a place where opportunities are limited. If you can do that in Marfa, imagine what's possible in Austin."

I'm seduced by his confidence in me, his obvious desire to work with me and his praise of what I've accomplished. There's something almost paternal about it that speaks to me in a place that's been hungry for paternal approval for six long, lonely years.

"Take a week… Hell, take two weeks if that's what you need. Think it over from every angle before you decide anything."

Now would be a great time to let him know I've decided to marry the love of my life, who owns a thriving business of her own in Marfa and won't want to move to Austin, or anywhere else for that matter. But even as the thoughts swirl through my mind, I can't bring myself to turn him down when he's sitting three feet from me.

"My wife, Monica, and I are looking forward to taking you and your friend to dinner tonight. We have seven o'clock reservations at the Austin Country Club. I hope that suits you."

I should tell him that Lauren is my fiancée, not just my friend. "It sounds great. If I could ask a favor, though."

"Of course."

"Could we keep dinner strictly social? I need some time to talk to Lauren about your offer."

"Absolutely. That's no problem at all."

"Thank you for everything. You've definitely given me plenty to think about."

"Excellent. Is there anything you'd like to do while you're here? I can get you tickets to just about anything."

"There is one thing I'd love to do."

"Name it."

"I need an engagement ring."

His face lights up with delight. "Congratulations."

"Thank you."

"I have just the guy." He withdraws his cell phone and scrolls through his contacts before placing a call. "Henry, it's Jerry. I have a colleague in town who's in need of an engagement ring. Can you fit him in this afternoon?" He listens for a brief moment and then nods. "Perfect. I'll send Mr. Garrett McKinley right over. Thanks a lot." After he ends the call, he says, "I'll have the driver take you there on the way back to the hotel, if that works for you."

As someone who admires people who get shit done, I'm as impressed by him as I was by the rest of his team. The tone at the top clearly resonates in this company. "That works for me. Appreciate that and everything else." With the folder containing the offer in hand, I rise to leave his office.

He walks me to the elevator and shakes my hand. "I'll see you tonight."

"Yes, I'll see you then. Thank you again for an incredible day."

"It was our pleasure."

On the elevator ride to the lobby, I find myself thinking about a trip my family took to Galveston when I was about eight. Lola was a toddler, and my mom was pregnant with Sierra. Tommy, Colby and I loved our first visit to the beach and had spent hours digging holes and filling them with water under the watchful eye of our father. We spent a week there, and every day we became more brazen and fearless around the water as only boys who don't know better can do.

On the last day, I got caught in a rip current that dragged me out so fast that I didn't have time to react before I was in water over my head. I can still remember the moment when I realized I was in big trouble and the sheer panic that had gripped me before my dad reached me and saved me from going under.

The only other time I've ever felt panic quite like that was years later when he died and I was forced to pick up the reins at the business that supported us all. In the elevator with Dutton's million-dollar offer with stock options tucked under my arm, my chest constricts with the same sense of panic I've experienced twice before.

I never should've come here. I shouldn't have let them show me what might've been. I was far better off not knowing.

The driver is waiting for me outside and opens the door to the black Cadillac sedan. "I trust you had a nice day, sir."

"I did. Thank you."

He drives a short distance before taking a series of turns that deposits us into a nondescript parking lot. He points to a door. "Ring the bell. They're expecting you."

"Thank you."

"My pleasure, sir."

I ring the bell and wait less than a minute before the door opens to admit me into a room that looks more like someone's parlor than a retail store. I'm offered refreshments, which I decline. Less than five minutes later, a man in a black suit comes into the room carrying several cases that he places on the table before extending his hand. "Mr. McKinley, I'm Henry Banks."

I shake his hand. "Thank you for seeing me on such short notice."

"Any friend of Jerry Dutton's is a friend of mine. I understand you're in the market for an engagement ring."

"That's right."

"Who's the lucky lady? Tell me a little about her."

How to summarize the magic that is Lauren in a few words? "Lauren is... She's sweet and fiercely loyal to the people she loves. She's tough on the outside but soft on the inside." Once again, a swell of emotion takes me by surprise and leaves a lump in my throat. I ought to be used to that after the overabundance of feelings I've had for her lately, but it still catches me off guard every time. "She has the biggest heart and is a talented florist and... She's been my very best friend since we were in the sixth grade."

"You know what I love about your description?"

I clear the lump of emotion from my throat. "What's that?"

"You never mentioned her physical appearance. Most guys I work with start with appearance when I ask them that question. I like to think it's a sign of a successful union when how she looks is the last thing you think of when describing the woman you love."

His comment pleases me. I like to think our union will be successful. I can't imagine any other outcome for us. "Just to be clear," I say with a smile, "she's stunningly beautiful."

He returns my smile. "I had no doubt. Let's find something as beautiful as she is to seal the deal, shall we?"

"Yes, please."

*

An hour later, I leave the jewelers with a three-carat diamond ring and a staggering array of information about diamond clarity, cut, carat and color. I want only the best for Lauren, so I took my time deciding on a solitaire with a wraparound band of smaller diamonds. Because I want her to be able to wear it all the time, even when she's working, I was careful to ensure the stone is serviceable and won't catch on everything that it comes into contact with.

I can't wait to give it to her and see her eyes light up with joy. Anticipating that reaction makes my heartbeat quicken and my body tingle with love and desire and excitement for what's ahead for us.

When I get back to Marfa, I'll let Jerry know that as dazzled as I am by his company—and him—I have to pass on his generous offer. My life—and Lauren's—is in Marfa, and that's where we'll be staying after we're married. It was nice to be wanted, to be courted, to recall a time in my life when anything was possible. But I've moved on. I have a thriving business with clients who need me and employees who depend upon me. While I was busy feeling trapped in Marfa, I was also building a life there that has become a thousand times more satisfying now that Lauren and I are an official couple.

I can picture our life there in a way that I couldn't even two weeks ago. Having her by my side and in my bed has silenced the disquiet I've lived with since I was forced to come home to take over my father's business. The bitterness is gone. The resentment is gone. The craving need for something else, something *better*, is gone. I'm finally content, and it's all because of her.

The driver drops me off at the main entrance to the hotel and tells me he'll be back to collect us for dinner at six forty-five.

"I'll see you then," I say as I head into the lobby, checking my watch to see that we have two hours until our pickup. That ought to be just enough time for what I have in mind. I can't wait to hear what she thought of the spa and whether she got to the pool. On the way home to Marfa tomorrow, I'll tell her the truth about why we came here and what I've discovered as a result. I'll have to frame it in such a way that she understands I was merely testing the waters, not actually planning to leave Marfa.

I'll tell her everything about how I really felt about inheriting the family business and having to put my own ambitions on hold for all this time. I'm sure she'll understand my need for closure, or at least I hope she will. Underneath my determination to be truthful with her is a gnawing fear that hearing I'd gone so far as to engage a headhunter and attend an interview in Austin without telling her about it will hurt her. Hopefully, it'll make a difference when I tell her I've never spoken about any of this with anyone. For some reason, I'm oddly fearful of sharing this information with her, but I shake off those unsettling thoughts to focus on happier things like giving her the ring I chose for her.

I enter the suite and immediately remove my tie and suit coat, laying them both over a chair in the salon before going into the bedroom, where Lauren is curled into a little ball in the middle of the big bed, fast asleep. I take a minute to just drink her in while recalling my description of her as tough on the outside but soft on the inside.

She's wearing one of the thick white robes provided by the hotel, and I notice her toenails have been painted bright red at some point during the hours we spent apart. I debate whether I should let her sleep or let her know I'm back. I decide on a compromise, and after placing the ring box on the bedside table, I unbutton my shirt, pull it off and then remove my shoes, socks and suit pants. I crawl in next to her, wrapping my arm around her waist and breathing in a delicious new scent that I assume is from the spa. It's oaky and earthy with overtones of eucalyptus maybe. Whatever it is, my cock most definitely approves.

Because I can't help myself, I carefully untie the belt that's cinched around her waist and dip my hand inside to lie flat against the warm, silky skin on her belly. Of course that's not nearly enough, so I smooth my hand up until I encounter soft, pliable breast. She comes to when I run my thumb over the hardened tip of her nipple.

"I really hope you're Garrett, or I'm in big trouble," she says in a husky, sexy voice that goes straight to my already-hard cock.

"Who else would it be?"

"There was this really sexy bellman who caught my eye earlier."

I pinch her nipple hard enough to get her attention without causing actual pain. She giggles, and I smile at the sound of her laughter.

"How was your day, dear?" I ask.

"*De*lightful. Yours?"

"It was good, but it just got a whole lot better. You smell amazing, and your skin is like silk."

"I was very thoroughly pampered."

"That's great, sweetheart. You deserve it."

"I don't know about that, but I sure did love it. Thanks for inviting me."

"Thanks for coming with me. It wouldn't have been any fun without you."

"What time is dinner?"

"Our pickup is in two hours. I set the alarm on my phone for thirty minutes before so we don't have to watch the clock."

"What do you feel like doing until then? You want to go to the pool or take a nap or what?"

She's given me the perfect opening for what I want to do.

"Stay right there for a minute." I remove my hand from inside her robe and retrieve the ring box from the bedside table. "Turn over."

She gathers the two sides of the robe in her hand as she turns toward me. Her face is adorably flushed from sleep, and I have to kiss her, just once. Once becomes twice when her hand lands on my face, disarming me with her sweetness.

"Hi there," she says with a sexy smile.

"Hi." I kiss her again. "Missed you today."

"Mmm, me, too, but I was kept very well occupied while you were gone."

I narrow my brows. "Tell me your masseuse wasn't a guy."

"Um, well, I hate to tell lies…"

What does it say about how far gone I am over her that the thought of another man's hands on her, even in a professional capacity, infuriates me?

"So I can't tell you that my masseuse was a guy because *he* was a *she*."

I breathe a sigh of relief. "It's a good thing. I'd hate to have to hunt him down and kick his ass for daring to put his hands on my woman."

"Down, boy. It's all good."

"Is it? Are you happy, Lo?"

"How can you ask me that?" She strokes my face tenderly, her fingertips sliding over my skin. "I'm so happy. All day today, I just kept thinking about last night and the things we talked about, the plans we made. I can't believe this is happening."

"Believe it. It's happening, and so is this." I open my hand to reveal the black velvet box.

Her eyes widen and then fill with tears. "Garrett..."

"Open it."

She looks up at me, almost as if she's making sure I'm for real and then takes the box, her hand trembling ever so slightly. "I need to sit up for this." As she does, the robe falls open, revealing the deep valley between her breasts. I don't allow myself to be sidetracked. I keep my attention on her face, which lights up with pleasure at the sight of the ring I've chosen for her.

Tears flood her eyes and spill down her cheeks as she stares at it.

"You like it?"

She laughs and uses the sleeve of the robe to mop up her tears. "Of course I do. It's incredible."

I rise to my knees, take the box from her and raise my hand to her face. "Lauren Davies, love of my life since the sixth grade, will you do me the enormous honor of being my wife?"

"*Yes*," she says through more tears. She throws herself at me, but I'm ready for her, catching her and holding her tight against me.

"Are you sure?" I ask teasingly.

"I'm very, *very* sure. Are you?"

Gazing down at her lovely tearstained face, I've never been more sure of anything in my entire life. "Yeah, baby. I'm sure." I kiss her while working the ring free of the box behind her back. I break the kiss but only so I can slide the ring onto her left hand. I guessed at the size, and I'm relieved to see that I got it right. It's a perfect fit.

"It's so beautiful," she whispers.

"I'm glad you like it."

"I love it, but are you sure it's not too much? I don't need—"

I kiss the words right off her lips. "It's the ring I want you to have, but only if you're happy with it."

"I'm happy. I'm very happy."

"Then I am, too." I lie back down and invite her to join me, watching as she shimmies out of the robe and tosses it aside. As I put my arm around her, I say, "Wait until everyone at home hears our news."

"I don't think they'll be that surprised."

"No?"

She shakes her head and looks up at me. "According to Honey, they've been waiting for us to figure out that we're meant to be."

"Seriously?" I ask, astounded.

"Uh-huh. Apparently, we finish each other's sentences, always sit together in a group and laugh at the same things. You hold doors for me and generally dote on me."

"I do?"

"You do, and I'm not the only one who's noticed."

"Do you think it's weird that it took us so long to get to where we are now?"

"No, I think it was our journey, and it unfolded the way it was meant to. I wouldn't have been ready for this before now, and I suspect you wouldn't have been either."

"Probably not," I concede, turning so I'm on top of her, gazing down at her lovely face. "But I'm ready now."

"I can tell," she says with a saucy grin as she pushes her pelvis against my hard cock.

"Seriously, Lo. I'm ready for you, for us, for this. I love you so much. I always have, but now..."

"Now it's so much more," she says, finishing my sentence for me.

Nodding, I hold our eye contact as I kiss her, softly at first and then with greater desperation as the desire I'm learning to expect when we're together this way kicks in and takes over. It's so natural and easy with her. We move like we've been doing this for years rather than days.

I watch her face as I slide into her, moving slowly to draw out the anticipation for both of us. Her expression is so raw and unguarded and filled with love that's all for me. Her love has humbled me, made me want to be a better man so I'll always be worthy of the tremendous gift she's given me.

This, I realize in the midst of utter magic, is what it means to make love. I had no idea until I did this with her that there could be such a difference. I grasp her hands and prop them over her head, linking our fingers and then our lips as we ride the wave to a sharp peak and then glide back down together in a moment of the purest perfection I've ever experienced.

Her eyes are glossy with tears, her lips swollen from our kisses, and I'm completely lost to her in every possible way. Still joined with her, I move to my side and bring her with me, keeping her snug against me as our bodies cool and quake with aftershocks.

I should talk to her about what happened today, but I'm afraid to step outside the bubble of happy contentment that surrounds us. I want to preserve the perfection for as long as I can. There'll be time enough to talk it through tomorrow during the ride home.

CHAPTER 13

Lauren

Garrett's alarm wakes us thirty minutes before we're due to be picked up. Part of me wishes we didn't have to leave our bed or our room to be sociable, but he's here to meet with potential clients, and they were good enough to put us up at the Four Seasons for the weekend. After my amazing day at the spa, the least I can do is spend a few hours with them supporting his business.

I drag myself from his embrace and out of bed to put myself together.

He staggers into the bathroom a few minutes later, looking rumpled and sexy and sleepy. I can't take my eyes off the exceptional naked body of the man who will be my husband. My first and only love… At long last, we finally got the timing right.

He goes into the toilet room to take a leak that I can hear through the closed door. It's so intimate and exciting to be with him this way, to see him disheveled, to share a living space, even if it's a hotel room.

I hold out my hand to study the exquisitely beautiful engagement ring he gave me. He took me completely by surprise when he returned with the ring and officially asked me to marry him. If he had any idea how long I've waited to hear those words from him, he'd probably run away out of fear of a woman who was so crazy about him that, other than the very brief fling with Blake, she hasn't been with anyone else since she split with her husband years ago.

All those long years of waiting and hoping that Garrett McKinley might one day look at me as more than just a buddy. And then the first time he did, it was such an unmitigated disaster that I nearly gave up on us being anything more to each other than the best of friends.

His hands land on my hips, his chin on my shoulder. "You still like the ring in the bright light?"

"I love it in every light. I still can't believe we're actually engaged!"

He hugs me tighter against him. "Believe it."

"I might need to call Honey tonight rather than waiting until we get home to tell her."

"Whatever you want, sweetheart."

"I'm torn between wanting to tell her now and wanting to be there when she sees a ring on my finger."

"It would be fun to surprise them."

"Yes, it would. That's what we'll do. Somehow I'll find a way to contain myself until we get home."

"Share your excitement with me."

"I can do that." I catch his eye in the mirror. "Do you think your mom will be happy for us?"

"She'll be thrilled."

"I hope so. She's the only parent we have, the only grandparent our kids will have."

"She'll be a fantastic grandmother—and mother-in-law. You know how much she's always loved you."

"She's one of several people who saved me back in the day—her and Honey's Gran and a couple of teachers who actually gave a shit about me." I rub at the faded white scar on my left wrist that serves as a reminder of another of the dark times in my life, after I fended off the advances of one of my drunken, drugged-up mother's many "boyfriends," and then slashed my wrists in a desperate attempt to get someone to notice how neglected I was. It worked. After I ended up in the hospital, the state intervened to get me out of her home and helped me become an emancipated minor at the age of sixteen.

I stayed for a time with Honey and her Gran, the older woman who adopted her as an infant, before giving my mother another chance after she supposedly "got sober and found religion." That turned out to be a huge mistake. I married Wayne to finally get away from her, trading one awful situation for another. When I was twenty-four, my mother died in prison, a convicted drug dealer. I hadn't seen her in more than a year by then, but was still profoundly affected by her death.

"Don't think about the bad stuff, Lo," Garrett says, tugging my left arm free and encircling my wrist with his big hand. "It's all over now. Let's look ahead rather than back."

Nodding, I force a smile for his benefit. This is certainly not the time for that trip down memory lane. "I'll be ready in ten minutes."

"Sounds good." He kisses the back of my shoulder and leaves me to finish getting ready.

I want to look nice for him tonight so he'll be proud to introduce me to his clients, so I take special care with my hair, straightening the crazy curls and applying a little more makeup than I normally wear. I don a black cocktail dress and the super-high heels that Garrett likes so much. When I'm ready, I leave the bathroom and find him standing in front of the big windows in the salon, hands in his pockets as he gazes out at the view of Lady Bird Lake.

He's wearing a pinstripe dress shirt with black pants that mold to his perfect ass. I go to him and cover that tight ass with my hands, giving him a little squeeze that makes him jolt.

He smiles at me over his shoulder and then does a double take. "Wow, you look fantastic." Turning, he takes a closer look. "You look so different with your hair straight." He lets a strand slide through his fingers, seeming fascinated.

"Do you not like it?"

"I love it. You look sexy and grown up and engaged."

"I didn't know it was possible to look engaged."

"You do. You look very, *very* engaged, which is a good thing. I want everyone to know you belong to me."

I bring him in for a quick kiss. "You're very sweet."

"Let's go get this dinner over with so we can continue to properly celebrate our engagement." He takes me by the hand and grabs his suit coat on the way out of the suite.

The driver is waiting for us, and Garrett holds the door for me and then follows me into the back of the Cadillac for the ride to the Austin Country Club.

"Guests of Jerry Dutton," the driver tells the guard at the security station. We're waved in and given a VIP greeting by club staff. My first thought at watching them spring into action is that whoever Jerry Dutton is, he must have sway at this place.

We're shown to a table in the middle of an elegant dining room. A handsome man in his mid-fifties stands to greet Garrett with a big welcoming smile and a handshake.

"This is my fiancée, Lauren," Garrett says, and I have to make an effort not to swoon as I'm introduced as his fiancée for the first time.

"Such a pleasure to meet you," Jerry says. "This is my wife, Monica."

I shake hands with the stunning dark-haired woman with the perfect skin, teeth and manicure. She reminds me, oddly, of George Clooney's gorgeous wife, and next to her, I feel like a country bumpkin. I'm really glad I took the time to straighten my hair.

Garrett helps me into my chair and then takes the seat next to me, resting his hand on my thigh as if he knows I need the reassurance. I've got this, or so I tell myself. I'm determined not to do anything to embarrass him in front of these people. I have no idea what sort of work he's hoping to gain from Jerry Dutton, but whatever it is, it was important enough to drive six and a half hours to meet with him.

Jerry recommends the steak special, which Garrett and I order, while Monica orders something vegetarian. Of course she does.

I have a glass of red wine while Garrett drinks bourbon with Jerry and Monica orders white wine.

"A toast," Jerry says, "to new friends."

We touch our glasses together, and I sense a creeping tension in Garrett that wasn't there when we left the hotel room.

"So y'all are engaged," Monica says. "Show me your ring."

I raise my hand off my lap and extend it to her.

"That's gorgeous. Well done," she says to Garrett.

"Thank you."

"When's the big day?" she asks.

"Oh, we don't know yet," I say, glancing at Garrett. "We just got engaged."

"Just as in since you've been here?"

"Just as in this afternoon."

"Oh my goodness! Jerry, we need champagne! They just got engaged!"

Smiling indulgently at his wife, he raises a hand to summon the waiter and order champagne. "Bring us your best vintage."

"Yes, sir, Mr. Dutton. Coming right up."

"This is so exciting," Monica says, clapping her hands with girlish glee. She's a lot nicer than I expected her to be at first glance. "You have to tell us everything. How did you meet?"

I look to Garrett, who smiles and nods at me to tell our story. "We've known each other since kindergarten, but we've been close since sixth grade."

"Oh, that's so sweet! Isn't that sweet, Jerry?"

"Indeed," he says.

"Garrett came to my rescue when another boy knocked my lunch tray out of my hands."

"Bruce the Dick Dickenson," Garrett adds, making them laugh.

"Garrett beat the crap out of him, got suspended and we've been the best of friends ever since." I grasp his hand under the table. "The romantic part is more recent, but it's been a long time coming."

"A very long time," he murmurs, squeezing my hand. "Too long."

"You have to invite us to the wedding," Monica says.

"Monica," Jerry says with a note of warning in his voice. "Don't be pushy."

"Am I being pushy, Lauren?"

"Not at all," I say, charmed by her over-the-top friendliness. "Of course we'll invite you, and you can drive six and a half hours to the middle of nowhere Texas for the wedding."

"I love seeing new places," Monica says. "It's always an adventure."

Dinner is a great time, full of lively conversation and laughter, topped off with a delicious meal. The guys have obviously made a pact to not discuss business, which is fine with me.

"I need to hit the ladies' room," Monica says after our dinner dishes are cleared. Looking over at me, she says, "Join me?"

"Sure."

Both men get up to help us out of our chairs, and Monica links her arm through mine as she leads the way to the restroom. "Y'all are just too damned cute," she says once we're inside the room that looks more like a fancy Southern parlor than a bathroom. "He's a sexy one, that man of yours."

"I agree."

"You're a lucky girl."

"As are you. Jerry is a sweetheart."

"He certainly is."

We take care of business and then meet again at the mirror to refresh lipstick.

"Jerry made me promise no talk of business tonight, but I have to tell you how excited we are about having you guys here with us in Austin. Jerry is just tickled pink to have found Garrett. I know nothing's decided yet, but I do hope we'll be the best of friends."

I have no idea what the hell she's talking about, and it takes a few seconds for her to realize that.

"Oh God. I've gone and put my foot right in it, haven't I?"

"I, um…" My recently satisfied stomach begins to ache, and for a second, I fear that I'm going to be sick right in the rarefied confines of the Austin Country Club ladies' room. "Will you please tell me what you're talking about?"

"I probably shouldn't. Jerry's going to kill me."

"Please, Monica."

She hesitates, but only for a moment. "Jerry is hoping to hire Garrett to be the new chief financial officer of his company. That's why y'all are here. He interviewed with Jerry and the team at the office today."

I feel like I've been punched right in the gut. He's here for an *interview* and didn't think I needed to know that? What the hell? What about my business? What about *his*? I'm reeling. My head is spinning as I try to make sense of it. Why would he keep such a thing from me? And is he planning to take the job and spring a move to Austin on me?

"I'm so sorry, Lauren," Monica says, blinking back tears. "I feel terrible."

"It's not your fault."

"I'm sure he has a good reason for not telling you."

What possible reason could he have for keeping such a big secret from me at the same time he was asking me to marry him? "I… I need a minute. If you don't mind."

"Of course, honey," she says, squeezing my arm. "Take all the time you need. I'll make excuses for you."

"Thank you."

She leaves me alone in the restroom, and I make use of one of the upholstered easy chairs to try to collect my thoughts. I'm there a few minutes before one thing becomes crystal clear to me. I need to get the hell out of here. Right now.

Garrett

Monica returns to the table alone and obviously distressed.

"Where's Lauren?" I ask.

To my astonishment—and apparently Jerry's, too—she becomes teary-eyed as she takes her seat at the table. "I've made a terrible faux pas."

My heart begins to pound erratically, and I break into a cold sweat.

"What've you done, darlin'?" Jerry asks.

"I mentioned how excited you are for Garrett to join the company and..."

I'm on my feet before she completes the sentence. "Where is she?"

"Still in the ladies' room."

I run toward the direction I saw them go when they left the table, and I bang on the door. "Lauren! Baby, come out here. Let me explain."

"Is there a problem, sir?" a uniformed guy asks.

"Yes, there's a very big problem. My fiancée is in there, and she thinks I did something that I didn't mean to do, and I need to talk to her. Right now."

The door opens, and an irritated older woman comes out. "What seems to be the problem?"

"My fiancée is in there." I'm feeling more desperate by the minute. "I need to talk to her. Will you ask her to come out?"

"I was the only one in there."

"You're sure?"

"Positive."

I run for the foyer and the portico where my driver stands with several other men. "Did you see Lauren? The woman I was with earlier?"

"She left a few minutes ago in one of the club's cars," he says. "Said she had a headache and that I should wait for you to conclude your business."

"I need to get back to the hotel. Right now."

"Yes, sir." He signals for the valet, and we wait an interminable ten minutes for them to bring the car around. When he starts to come back to hold the door for me, I signal for him to skip that. "Drive as fast as you can. Get me to the hotel."

When we're in the car, I try to call her, but I get her voice mail, which means her phone is off. I'm losing my mind on the ride back to the hotel, imagining what she must be thinking and how upset she had to be to leave without a word to me.

It's the least of what I deserve. I fucked this up royally, even if my intentions were good.

At the hotel, I'm out of the car before it comes to a full stop and run into the lobby, punching the up arrow on the elevator repeatedly until a car finally arrives. I drop the fucking keycard in my haste to get to the top floor, losing another valuable minute. Finally, I get to our room and open the door, yelling her name to an empty suite.

She's not there.

I go to the closet and throw it open to find her bag is gone along with her cosmetic bag from the counter in the bathroom.

"*Fuck!* Motherfucking *fuck!*"

I call downstairs for my car, throw my stuff into my suitcase and leave the room five minutes after I arrived. I have no desire to be there for even a minute if she's not with me.

At the bellman's station, I describe her to the man on duty and ask if he's seen her. "I saw her. About ten minutes ago. She hired one of the car service guys to take her home to someplace in the desert."

"Marfa."

"Yeah, that's it. The driver was thrilled with the big fare."

I'm going to be sick. The nausea burns my throat and brings tears to my eyes. My phone rings, and I take the call from Jerry Dutton.

"Is everything all right, Garrett?" he asks.

"Not really, but hopefully it will be." I can't consider the alternative.

"Monica feels terrible."

"Please tell her it's not her fault. It's one hundred percent mine. I hadn't told Lauren why we were really here because I'd decided not to accept the job, but after you all went to so much trouble to set things up, I wanted to at least meet with you."

"Well, I have to say that's very disappointing. We all felt you'd be a perfect fit for the job."

"Maybe in another lifetime," I say as the valet arrives with my car. I slip him a ten, throw my bag into the front seat, hit the gas and head for home. "In this lifetime, I belong somewhere else entirely. I'm sorry to have led you on, Jerry. I never meant for that to happen."

"Ahh, don't sweat it. Shit happens. My door is always open to you, Garrett. If you change your mind, you know where I am."

"I appreciate that and everything else."

"No problem. I hope things work out for you and Lauren."

"So do I." We end the call as I get on the interstate and press the gas pedal to the floor. Thank goodness I had only one glass of bourbon with dinner, because this is going to be a long night.

I try to see inside every car I pass on the long ride home, but I never catch a glimpse of anything resembling Lauren's distinctive blonde hair. I reach the outskirts of Marfa around two a.m., having had to stop twice—once for gas and once to piss. I'm hovering on the razor's edge of sanity by the time I drive down Highland and notice her car is no longer in the lot where we left it on Friday. That means she made it back to town before me, although how that's possible with the way I drove is beyond me.

I'm on the way to her house when my phone rings. I pounce on it without checking the caller ID.

"It's Blake."

I deflate like a balloon that's been hit with a pin.

"Honey's in labor. We're at Big Bend in Alpine."

"Does Lauren know?"

"I just talked to her a few minutes ago because Honey asked me to call her. She said she's home, but she didn't know where you are. What the hell is going on, man?"

"Don't sweat it. Focus on your wife and your baby."

"Garrett—"

"I'm coming there. See you in thirty minutes." I end the call before he can grill me any further. At least now I know where to find Lauren.

CHAPTER 14

Garrett

Thirty minutes later, I pull into the parking lot at the Big Bend Regional Medical Center in Alpine, the closest thing to a hospital in our neck of the woods. I run inside, fueled by adrenaline and panic, and immediately see Lauren sitting with Scarlett and a big blond guy I don't recognize in the waiting room.

"Lauren." The single word sounds almost like a sob as it leaves my mouth.

She looks up at me, and in the flash of an instant, I see hurt and disappointment and disaster. I also notice she's not wearing her ring.

"I need to talk to you."

"Not now."

"Lauren, please…"

Scarlett and the blond guy watch us with curiosity from him and dismay from her.

Lauren glares at me. "Not. Now. *Garrett.*"

I want to fucking punch something, but I restrain that urge and force myself to calm the fuck down before I make this worse, if that's even possible. I take a seat across from her and train my gaze on her, which is how I know that she never once looks my way in the two hours we wait to hear that Blake and Honey's son has arrived safely.

Wyatt James Dempsey is born at four seventeen a.m., weighing just over nine pounds and measuring twenty-one inches. According to his euphoric father, his mother is a warrior and the baby is a future linebacker. I've never seen Blake so happy in all the years I've known him, and he's been pretty damned happy since he got together with Honey.

Did I have that kind of happiness in my grasp until I fucked it up and ruined everything?

They let us in to see Honey and the baby a little while later. I remind myself to say and do all the right things to support my friends, but I'm dying on the inside with the need for five minutes alone with Lauren to fix this terrible mess I've made of things.

It turns out the big blond guy is Mickey's brother Jace, who was with Blake when Honey went into labor.

"I'm glad you guys got the chance to meet," Blake says while the women coo over the baby. "Garrett runs my business."

"Ask him how he plans to run your business from Austin," Lauren says, dropping a bomb into the room.

"You wanna run that by me one more time?" Blake says to her.

"Tell him, Garrett. Tell him about the interview you had in Austin to be the chief financial officer at Social-NET." She must've Googled Jerry Dutton on the way home. "You know, the interview you didn't tell anyone about, even me, when you were asking me to marry you?"

"You guys are *engaged*?" Scarlett says with a squeal that startles the baby.

"We *were*," Lauren says.

"We *are*," I confirm with a steady look for her. "The job thing is all a big misunderstanding."

She stares me down. "Did you or did you not go to Austin for a job interview?"

"I did, but—"

"No buts! You were making plans to leave town, and you didn't tell any of us!"

"Seriously, Garrett?" Blake says. "What the fuck?"

"Don't swear in front of the baby," Honey says. "But honestly, Garrett, what were you thinking? You know how much we all rely on you."

"If you guys would let me get a word in edgewise, I'd tell you that I took the meeting, but I never had any intention of taking the job."

"How did a company in Austin even know about you?" Blake asks.

"That's a very good question," Lauren says, "and one I'd like to know the answer to as well."

I'm cornered with no clean way out of this except with the truth. "In order for me to explain that to you, we'd have to go back to what I was doing when my father died."

"What does that have to do with this?" Honey asks, cradling the sleeping baby in her arms.

As much as I want to explain myself to them, I can't do it here or now. "Guys, really, this isn't the time or the place. We need to be focused on Wyatt and Honey and your new family." I go over to the bed and lean over to kiss Honey's forehead and run my finger over the baby's downy soft cheek. "Well done, Mom. I'm so happy for you guys."

"Thank you for being here, Garrett."

"Of course."

"Congratulations," I say to Blake, extending my hand to him.

He shakes my hand as he gives me a wary look. "This conversation isn't finished."

"We'll talk about it another time," I tell him.

"You bet your ass we will."

"Blake! Language!"

"Babe, we've got two years before he'll be able to talk."

"No time like the present to break the habit."

"Come with me," I say to Lauren.

"No, I'm staying with Honey."

"You don't have to, Lo," she says. "All I want to do is sleep. You don't have to stay."

"We'll all get out of your hair," Scarlett says. To Jace, she adds, "Can I hitch a ride back to town with you?"

"Of course. No problem." He shakes hands with Blake. "To be continued."

"Thanks an awful lot for everything tonight, man. If you want the job, it's all yours after what you did to get me to Honey when she needed me."

"I want the job, and it was a pleasure. Glad I could help and that I got to meet your friends." He waggles his eyes at Scarlett, who's oblivious because she's hugging Lauren and whispering something to her.

We walk out together, and I follow Lauren to her car.

"Come to my place," I say to her. "Let me explain."

"It's late, Garrett. I'm tired and—"

"Please, Lauren."

She sighs. "Fine. Okay."

The greatest feeling of relief I've ever experienced floods my system. We're not out of the woods yet, but at least she's going to hear me out. "Follow me."

With a curt nod, she gets in her car and pulls out of the parking lot right behind me. I lead the way back to Marfa and pull into my driveway, opening two of the garage doors so she can drive in next to me.

I close the doors and wait for her to precede me into the house. "You want something to drink?"

"Just some water."

I pour glasses of ice water for both of us and bring them into the living room, taking the seat next to her on the sofa. "The first thing I want to say is I'm sorry I didn't tell you why we really went to Austin."

"I've spent the last ten hours trying to understand why you didn't tell me."

"Like I said at the hospital, after everything clicked with us, I decided I didn't want the job after all, but Jerry and his team had gone to so much trouble to arrange everything, I didn't feel right canceling at the last minute. And then when Wayne showed up and upset you, I thought it would be a good chance to get you away from it all for a few days."

"Which was nice of you, and I appreciate it, but can you begin to understand how it felt to have someone I don't know at all fill in the blanks for me?"

"I'm sorry about that. Jerry and I had agreed this would be a social dinner with no business. I didn't think it would come up."

"Were you ever going to tell me that you went there for an interview?"

"I was planning to tell you about it on the way home, after I declined their offer."

"I'm having a hard time understanding why you had the interview in the first place if you didn't want the job."

"Like I said earlier, it goes back to what I was doing when my father died."

"What were you doing?"

"Interviewing with companies just like Jerry's, places with lots of opportunities and offices around the world."

In the span of one second, I watch as she puts it all together. "So you've been counting down the days until Sierra graduates so you can get back to what you were doing before your dad died?"

"Not the whole time."

"Oh my *God*, Garrett." She bends in half as if in pain, rocking back and forth. "All these years… How could you not tell me you wanted to be somewhere else? What did you think I would say?"

"It's not like that, Lo. I was only exploring my options."

"What about your clients here? People like Blake and Honey who depend on you? What were you going to say to them on your way out of town?"

"I would've provided for them and my employees. But it doesn't matter anymore. I'm not going anywhere. I want something different now." I reach for her hand, which is freezing, so I rub it between both of mine. "Why did you leave me in Austin?"

"I was shocked by what Monica told me. I just needed to get out of there."

"Without me?"

"I didn't know what to think. Why hadn't you told me about the interview? Were you planning to spring a move on me without a care about my life or my business? Do I even know the guy I was engaged to?"

"Past tense? Seriously, Lauren?"

"I don't know!" She pulls her hand free of my grasp and gets up to pace. "I don't understand any of this. How could I not know that you're so unhappy here? Even before this." She waves her hand between us. "We were together all the time, and I never had any idea that you were dying to be somewhere else."

"I wasn't. Not all the time."

"But most of the time. This is the reason why you never allowed yourself to have a relationship with anyone, because you were planning to leave. It's why you were so fond of tourists, isn't it? You were always planning your great escape."

"Everything is different now. Because of you and us."

"You want me to believe that you're prepared to abandon your life plan of more than six years after *one week* with me?"

"I'm in love with you. I want a life with you. I want that more than I've ever wanted anything else."

"So you say now. What about in a year or two or three when the excitement wears off and real life sets in and you start to feel unfulfilled?"

I get up and go to her, putting my arms around her rigid body. "If I have you in my life and in my bed, I'll never be unfulfilled. Don't you get it, Lauren? I wanted all that because my life was so empty, and now it's full to overflowing because of *you*. Loving you, being in love with you, has changed everything. The only thing I want now is you. I don't care where we are or where we live or what else happens as long as I have *you*."

I tug her closer, nuzzling her neck and breathing in the scent that's so uniquely Lauren. "I love you. I want you. I choose you. I didn't tell you about the interview because I wanted you to have a stress-free getaway. I never wanted you to know that I ever thought about being anywhere but here with you. I just wanted to get you away from here for a few days so you could relax after what happened with Wayne. I'm sorry you were hurt by something I failed to do. I'll never forgive myself for that."

Slowly, she begins to yield to me, her body molding to mine in tiny increments.

"That's it, baby. Come to me. Hold on to me. I'll never let you go." I feel dampness against my face and draw back to look down at her. I die inside at the sight of her tears, knowing I caused them.

"C-could I ask you something?"

"Anything."

"Did it ever occur to you that I might be willing to move to Austin if you got a job there that you're excited about?"

I stare down at her, stunned by the question. "No. That never occurred to me. I know how hard you've worked to build Bloomsbury and how much you love your friends and your life here. I'd never ask you to give any of that up for me."

"What if I was willing to do that for you if it's what would make you happy?"

"I don't need it, Lo. I have a wonderful, thriving business here with clients who rely on me as well as a woman I love and want to marry. My mom is here. My siblings are around at various times during the year. And my friends are here. While I was busy running my father's business, I found a life that works for me. The headhunter and the interview were leftover relics from an old dream. One that died a long time ago without me realizing it."

"I want to believe everything you're saying, but I'm afraid."

"Tell me why."

"I'd never want to hold you back from being everything you ever dreamed of being. Someday you'd resent me for that."

"You're not holding me back. Your love gave me the courage to trade one dream for an even better one. What would I do in Austin without you? I wouldn't last a month if I couldn't see your gorgeous face and kiss your sweet lips every day. You've got me completely addicted to you."

"You're one thousand percent sure this is what you want?"

"I'm one hundred million percent sure." Tipping my head to the side, I bring my lips down on hers, sliding them back and forth until I feel her yield to me, the breath escaping from her in an unsteady hitch. "I love you with my whole heart and soul, Lauren, and I have since the day Bruce the Dick made you cry. Tell me you still love me."

"I do. Of course, I do."

"Where's your ring?"

"In my purse."

"Go get it." Even though I never want to let her go, I release her so she can cross the room to the counter where she left her purse. She returns to me with the ring in hand and holds it up for me to see.

I take it from her and slide it back on her finger where it belongs. "Promise you'll never run away from me again. No matter what, run *to* me, not away."

"I promise."

"And I promise to never again give you reason to want to run." I wrap my arms around her and lift her into my embrace, carrying her to bed as the sun begins to peek through the blinds. Thank God we're both off on Sundays, or I'd have to miss work again to spend the day with my fiancée. The greatest thrill of my life is making love to her with no secrets left between us, and our future together laid out before us like a dream come true.

EPILOGUE

Garrett

"Who decided that babies have to wear frilly dresses to be christened?" Blake asks, curling his lip with distaste at the lacy outfit his son is currently wearing. "My son does not wear dresses. Even to church."

"It was Gran's," Honey says, pacifying him with a smile. "I'm going to change him now that we're home."

"Thank God. I need a beer. Who's in?"

Matt, Jace, Brock and I follow him to the bar that's been set up in the dining room for the party to celebrate Wyatt's christening. Lauren and I are his godparents, which turned out to be far more thrilling than I would've expected before I stood up in church and promised to be an important person in his new life.

Because Matt's arms are full of a squirming baby Grace, I open his beer and hand it to him.

"Thanks, pal," he says.

Honey comes into the dining room with Wyatt changed into a cute red polo shirt and khaki shorts and hands him to his father.

"Now that's more like it, my little man. I won't let Mommy do anything like that to you again. Don't worry."

"You are far too macho for your own good, Blake Dempsey," Honey says over her shoulder as she heads for the kitchen.

"I'm with you," Jace says. "The dress was a little much."

In two months, he's become part of our tribe and has completely transformed Blake's business with his construction management expertise. Not to mention the significant chemistry we've witnessed between him and Scarlett, which neither of them is talking about—not to us anyway.

"The christening gown has been in Gran's family for generations," Blake says with a long-suffering sigh. "It was important to Honey that he wear it, but I'm glad to see him out of it, too."

"He's cute no matter what he wears," I say with godfatherly pride.

"Isn't he?" Blake beams at his son with what can only be called unfettered joy. Honey and the baby have made him so damned happy.

We enjoy a feast of barbecue and all the fixings to celebrate Wyatt's baptism. Lauren sits beside me, her leg snug against mine while my hand rests on her thigh. I can't sit this close to her and not touch her. In the last few months, we've sold my house and moved me into hers. She was more attached to hers than I was to mine, so it was a no-brainer for me. Whatever she wants. In fact, if she had any idea how enslaved I am to her, I'd be in even bigger trouble than I already am where she's concerned.

Ironically, since I took the option of leaving town off the table, my business has grown even more, thanks in large part to Jerry Dutton, who convinced me to consult for him on an informal basis. That takes me to Austin about once a month to do work I truly enjoy with a man who's become a friend. Funny how life works itself out, isn't it?

More than anything, my relationship with Lauren has made my life complete in ways I never could've imagined. Knowing she belongs to me and I belong to her is really and truly the only thing I need to be happy.

Sometimes I'm still amazed at how falling in love with her completely changed my life and gave me a whole new set of dreams that are way better than anything I could've hoped for if left to my own devices. Together we're a thousand times more than we were on our own.

We're getting married in the spring at the Paisano, but that'll be a formality. We're already married in all the ways that matter most, and I can't wait for the forever I get to spend with her. We've even asked Blake to build one of the new houses in his development for us. Oh, and another great part of my new life? I take weekends off now so I can spend every possible minute with Lauren.

Life is good and getting better all the time—and it's all because of, the girl I fell in love with in sixth grade.

***

Thank you for reading *Sex God*! I hope you loved Garrett and Lauren's story as much as I loved writing it. Being a writer is weird sometimes. I had no plans to write this book until Garrett started talking to me, demanding I get his funny words on the page and figure out his situation once and for all. I'm enjoying writing in this world of Marfa and West Texas, and I hope to revisit it again in the future when another of the characters starts whispering in my ear.

Make sure you're on my newsletter mailing list at marieforce.com to never miss a new book, a sale or an appearance in your area. Join the *Sex God* Reader's Group on Facebook at https://www.facebook.com/groups/SexGodReader/ to discuss the story with others!

As always, my thanks to my HTJB team who make it all happen—Julie Cupp, Lisa Cafferty, Holly Sullivan, Isabel Sullivan, Nikki Colquhoun and Cheryl Serra. Thank you to my awesome editorial team of Linda Ingmanson and Joyce Lamb as well as my beta readers, Anne Woodall and Kara Conrad, and my publicist Jessica Estep at InkSlinger PR. I so appreciate all of you!

Special thanks to my readers who follow me wherever the muse decides to take us on this crazy journey. Thank you for your love and support!

xoxo

Marie

OTHER TITLES BY MARIE FORCE

Other Contemporary Romances Available from Marie Force:

The Gansett Island Series

Book 1: Maid for Love

Book 2: Fool for Love

Book 3: Ready for Love

Book 4: Falling for Love

Book 5: Hoping for Love

Book 6: Season for Love

Book 7: Longing for Love

Book 8: Waiting for Love

Book 9: Time for Love

Book 10: Meant for Love

Book 10.5: Chance for Love, *A Gansett Island Novella*

Book 11: Gansett After Dark

Book 12: Kisses After Dark

Book 13: Love After Dark

Book 14: Celebration After Dark

Book 15: Desire After Dark

Book 16: Light After Dark

Gansett Island Episodes, Episode 1: Victoria & Shannon

Books from M. S. Force
The Erotic Quantum Trilogy
Book 1: Virtuous

Book 2: Valorous

Book 3: Victorious

Book 4: Rapturous

Book 5: Ravenous

Book 6: Delirious

Romantic Suspense Novels Available from Marie Force:
The Fatal Series
One Night With You, *A Fatal Series Prequel Novella*

Book 1: Fatal Affair

Book 2: Fatal Justice

Book 3: Fatal Consequences

Book 3.5: Fatal Destiny, *the Wedding Novella*

Book 4: Fatal Flaw

Book 5: Fatal Deception

Book 6: Fatal Mistake

Book 7: Fatal Jeopardy

Book 8: Fatal Scandal

Book 9: Fatal Frenzy

Book 10: Fatal Identity

Book 11: Fatal Threat

Single Title
The Wreck

ABOUT THE AUTHOR

Marie Force is the *New York Times* bestselling author of more than 50 contemporary romances, including the Gansett Island Series, which has sold nearly 3 million books, and the Fatal Series from Harlequin Books, which has sold 1.5 million books. In addition, she is the author of the Butler, Vermont Series, the Green Mountain Series and the erotic romance Quantum Series, written under the slightly modified name of M.S. Force. All together, her books have sold more than 5.5 million copies worldwide!

Her goals in life are simple—to finish raising two happy, healthy, productive young adults, to keep writing books for as long as she possibly can and to never be on a flight that makes the news.

Join Marie's mailing list for news about new books and upcoming appearances in your area. Follow her on Facebook at https://www.facebook.com/MarieForceAuthor, Twitter @marieforce and on Instagram at https://instagram.com/marieforceauthor/. Join one of Marie's many reader groups. Contact Marie at *marie@marieforce.com.*

63443651R00105

Made in the USA
Lexington, KY
07 May 2017